DIGGING HIS OWN GRAVE

Longarm had to laugh as he saw why he was still alive while Skippy and Percival were not. Sand had described Shadow Manners as tall and slender, wearing a suit under a Mexican sombrero. Nobody had told Alejandro to kill a tall, slender galoot wearing Army riding pants and a denim jacket under a Kansas farm boy's straw.

But the scene in the dimly lit barn got more serious as the one they called Ryan handed him a long-handled digging spade and muttered, "Get cracking."

Longarm jumped down into the hole with the shovel as he held his palmed derringer between the shovel shaft and his sweating fist. He had just two shots to back his play in the tricky light. Stalling for time, Longarm asked mildly, even as he started to dig, whether Alejandro had considered how such a generous boss meant to pay him and his own boys off once they were done here.

Alejandro soberly replied, "Keep digging and let us worry about the future, *mariposa mia*. Is nothing personal, but you will not be there for to see how this all turns out . . ."

➤ TABOR EVANS ◄

LONGARM

AND THE
OUTLAW'S SHADOW

J

JOVE BOOKS, NEW YORK

This is a work of fiction. Names, characters, places, and incidents either
are the product of the author's imagination or are used fictitiously,
and any resemblance to actual persons living or dead, business
establishments, events, or locales is entirely coincidental.

LONGARM AND THE OUTLAW'S SHADOW

A Jove Book / published by arrangement with
the author

PRINTING HISTORY
Jove edition / June 2004

Copyright © 2004 by Penguin Group (USA) Inc.

For information address: The Berkley Publishing Group,
a division of Penguin Group (USA) Inc.,
375 Hudson Street, New York, New York 10014.

ISBN: 0-515-13751-0

A JOVE BOOK®
Jove Books are published by The Berkley Publishing Group,
a division of Penguin Group (USA) Inc.,
375 Hudson Street, New York, New York 10014.
JOVE and the "J" design
are trademarks belonging to Penguin Group (USA) Inc.

PRINTED IN THE UNITED STATES OF AMERICA

10 9 8 7 6 5 4 3 2 1

Chapter 1

It rarely rained along the Jornado del Muerto. When it did, it made up for the long dry spells in between. So it was too noisy to chat aboard the northbound D&RG night flyer out of El Paso as they rattled and rolled through jet-blackness, punctuated by blinding lightning while serenaded by peals of thunder, gusting winds, lashing rain, and sheets of hailstones.

Deputy Marshal Custis Long of the Denver District Court didn't care. He felt no call to argue with the self-styled wrong man cuffed to his left wrist. He hadn't been the arresting officer. They'd sent him down to Texas to transport the federal prisoner back to Colorado on a charge of murder and armed robbery, and the protestations of innocence were more tedious than the swell gully-washer, which, with any luck, might last all night.

Longarm, as he was better known to readers of the *Rocky Mountain News* and along the Owlhoot Trail, had been warned never to play cards aboard a train with strangers called Doc. Nobody had said anything about strange-looking galoots dressed as ribbon clerks in suits and ties and big Mexican sombreros. So Longarm paid little mind to what seemed like a dentist on his way home under a border-town souvenir, swaying his way down the aisle in the smoke-filled gloom of the dimly lit passenger car, until all of a sudden the son of a bitch was slapping leather at point-blank range!

Caught off guard with his cross-draw .44-40 wedged between him and his prisoner, Longarm went for the vest-pocket derringer he packed for such occasions, numbly aware he was never going to make it as the muzzle of the stranger's own .44-40 was already rising to the occasion. But when the six-gun went off inches from Longarm's face, it was aimed at the bank robber seated to his left. So the prisoner jerked considerably as he took two hundred grains of hot lead in the chest more than once. Then the stranger with the funny hat dashed on past them to vanish between the cars. Longarm's hat fell off while he struggled to free himself from the limp weight of his dead prisoner. As he rolled to his own feet in the aisle, discarding the handcuff key in favor of his own six-gun, he staggered, and almost landed on his rump, when the train braked to a screeching stop on the wet steel tracks.

The rascal had pulled the emergency brake cord, Longarm knew as he regained his balance to chase after him. The platforms between cars were slippery with rain and half-melted hailstones, but Longarm managed to stay upright as he jumped off into darkness black as the pit, guided only by the sound of running footsteps off to the east of the tracks. He landed running in his own right until that other six-gun barked at him. Then he fired back at the muzzle flash and crabbed to one side.

The cuss never fired again. If he hadn't been hit, he'd been shown the distinct disadvantages of revealing one's position in a running gunfight after dark. And then the locomotive up the tracks a piece tooted twice and Longarm gasped, "Aw, shit!" as the train they'd just jumped off started up again.

Longarm knew the odds of catching up in time were slim, even if he'd been willing to let the man who'd assassinated his prisoner get away. So he soldiered on through the dark and stormy night, hatless and already soaked to the skin, in the direction where he'd last heard anything above the pelting rain, pounding hail, and gusting wind. A flash of lightning, too close for comfort, lit the surrounding desert up for the instant it took Longarm to spot what might have been a distant figure or a man-sized tree stump. So Longarm pegged a shot that way, and moved to one side as he reflected on how few trees grew along the Jornado del Muerto.

Nobody fired back. When he got about as far as where he might or might not have glimpsed something, there was nothing there, and Longarm wasn't too certain of his bearings now. So he stopped where he was, to stand in thought as the wind and rain tried to stagger him.

The hail, praise the Lord, had let up for the time being, and way off to the northeast shone a light in the dark. A lamp or maybe a candle in a window over yonder, depending on how far.

Since he had to head somewhere, Longarm headed for the distant mysterious light. What it was doing over yonder was the mystery. Nobody had much call to light anything along the Jornado del Muerto. Nobody lived there. Early Spanish explorers had dubbed the hundred-odd-by-forty-odd stretch of bleakness between the Caballos to the west and the San Andres to the east a "Journey of Death" because, like Death Valley, the Hastings Cutoff, and other apparent shortcuts leading far from water, the usually dry and dusty Jornado del Muerto could get mighty rough on daft critters needing more water than they could manage to haul.

3

The later mail routes and railroad had forged across the Jornado del Muerto to save many an arid mile along the north-south Rio Grande *east* of the Caballos, and practical Mexican riders had seeded the desert to either side of their Camino Real with dryland grass and weeds from Old Spain to take some of the sting out of a land even Mister Lo, the Poor Indian, had had no use for. But save for now-abandoned stagecoach relay stations fifteen or more miles apart, nobody was settled seriously along the Jornado del Muerto. So unless some homesteaders had gone *loco en la cabeza,* the odds were that that distant light in some distant window had been lit to guide a killer off a braked train safely home to some hideout!

The wind and rain never let up as Longarm slogged on toward whatever lay yonder. From time to time he found himself slogging through shin-deep running water. There were no creeks running seriously across the Jornado del Muerto, but rainwater had to run somewhere, and they called where it ran in such country "dry washes." He could make out the sounds of seriously running water ahead and slowed to pick his way with more care as he moved in on the mysterious light farther on.

Then the light winked out, winked on again, and then it seemed to be out. So Longarm pegged a shot at where it had been, heard a sharp coyote bark, and then the light was shining again.

Moving in with a wolfish grin, Longarm growled, "Let that be a lesson to you, Sneaky Pete. Never take a stand in the dark with a lamp lit on your far side!"

Edging ever closer with his eyes peeled and ears cocked in vain, he could almost feel the swift current of the wash ahead as he crunched down on what felt like tumbleweed. He hunkered for a feel with his free hand. It was that big straw sombrero. Edging forward, he felt the wet, gritty rim of the flooded wash beyond. Long-

4

arm whistled softly as he put things together and decided, "I winged you with that first shot. Otherwise, you would have felt tough enough to wade on across, and to hell with running water. You made your stand here, listening for my approach in the dark. I spotted you first and blew you out from under this swell hat. So Lord only knows how you'll wind up when all this water goes down again, dead or alive, and I ain't betting on a man hit at least twice and bobbing away in churning floodwater!"

Longarm put the broad-brimmed sombrero on. It helped a lot. He could already see better with less rain in the face. So the question before the house was where he wanted to head next.

He knew he'd come to the tracks of the D&RG if he just forged west. He knew that sooner or later the sun would come up again and he'd be in shape to flag down the first train that came along whether it was raining or not. He knew the smart thing to do, now that he'd nailed the one who'd killed his prisoner, would be to fold it for the night and come back with plenty of backup to scout for the assassin's body and possibly locate a hideout he'd never made it to.

Anybody could see that.

Longarm could still make out that distant light, and what were the odds of anybody being there by the time he could gather his own army?

Moving upstream a ways where the current might not be as strong, he headed across and soon saw why the other cuss had been stopped or turned back. Longarm was a strong man with long legs, but the inky rushing water was still waist-high in the middle and trying to wash the sand out from under his low-heeled army boots. He struggled to keep his footing and came close to losing it before he'd made it on across.

Slogging up the far bank, he loaded six in the wheel

as he moved in on whatever, wishing he had his sixteen-shot Winchester '73 with him. But what the hell, he was never likely to kiss Miss Ellen Terry, the most beautiful woman on the London stage, or appear on the cover of the *Illustrated Police Gazette*, either. So a man just had to make do with what he had to work with.

As he got closer, a lightning flash illuminated what looked to be the already crumbling 'dobe walls of a relay station for the coach line the Iron Horse had recently laid to rest forever. Somebody had salvaged the corral poles and front door. But there was enough of the tin roof left to keep the interior dry enough for that candle stuck in a bottle on a box.

Calling out in the name of the law could take as much as fifty years off the life of a man moving in on unknown quantities with a pistol. So Longarm circled in, trying to determine what he might be up against.

On the far side, under an overhang, Longarm spotted a mule team hitched to a covered surrey with its leather curtains down. Seeing no other riding stock, he muttered, "This must not be the place. Our pal wearing this hat was to meet somebody here after he'd shot that federal want, yanked the cord, and scooted off into the dark on foot. So where might the son of a bitch sent to meet him be?"

He moved around the rear of the surrey to follow the muzzle of his six-gun into the abandoned station. He almost jumped out of his skin, and he would have spun and fired, if the voice calling out to him hadn't been so polite and so female. He still threw down on the black leather curtains between them as the gal seated behind them called out, "Stop waving that fucking gun around and let's be on our way, Manners! We have to haul ass! What kept you? I heard that train stopping and starting again ages ago!"

Lowering his six-gun to a politer angle as the gal in

6

the driver's seat flapped the curtain between them open, Longarm tried, "I had to go 'round some floodwater. Nobody told me the creeks out here were fixing to rise tonight!"

She replied, "Get in. Put that fucking gun away. Who do you take me for, that Texas she-sheriff Ned Buntline wrote all those lies about? They told me they described me to you, Manners."

Longarm swung himself up beside her as he soberly replied, "They never told me you were this good-looking, ma'am."

It worked. The driver they'd sent to pick that killer up was not, as a matter of fact, bad-looking, as far as he could tell in such uncertain light. But when she gushed, "Aw, you don't have to butter me up!" Longarm knew she liked to be buttered up as most gals did.

Whoever she was, she snapped the ribbons and they drove out into the wind and rain. He started to ask a dumb question, but it was obvious the candle would go out when it burned down. It would have been dumber to ask her name, or what his own first name was supposed to be, now that she'd taken him for the Manners somebody had sent to murder his prisoner—the late Clem Aherne as that warrant had called him.

Manners had likely been instructed to meet whoever she was, while she in turn had been told to expect a tall galoot wearing a Mexican sombrero and packing a .44-40. But how far would it make sense to push such a freak of luck?

As they drove through the stormy night in the middle of nowhere, he could see it made more sense to get *somewhere* before he made any further moves. He saw he didn't have a good case against her or anybody else, except for a rascal he'd sent bobbing down a wash with at least two rounds in his likely dead hide. Where in the

Constitution did it say a lady couldn't offer a half-drowned stranger in the night a ride to somewhere better? Anywhere was better than a tumbledown ruin out on the Jornado del Muerto, and since she'd never known the real Manners, she could hardly know enough for him to haul her in kicking and screaming. It made more sense to let her take him closer, but not too close, to the bigger fish she and Manners had been recruited by.

He was dying to know where in blue thunder they could be headed. But since Manners would have likely known, he couldn't ask. He couldn't see shit ahead, but the team had to be following some sort of trail or trace.

As they rolled on, wet but warmer with the leather curtains between them and the wind and rain, she asked if it was safe to assume he'd shut Clem Aherne's big mouth for good. Longarm truthfully replied that the last he'd seen of old Clem, he had four rounds in his chest close enough together to cover with one ace of spades. She sounded impressed with him as she replied, "They said you had a steady gun hand. What about that famous lawman that was guarding Clem—Longarm, I think they call him?"

Longarm soberly replied, "He was caught asleep at the switch. Had his fool self handcuffed to a dead man before he could do anything famous. I was off the train and running too sudden to see just how they sorted things out back yonder."

She never asked about any gunshots. She'd likely taken any she might have heard for thunderbolts. She said, "Come daybreak your footprints across the desert pavement should be hard to read. If they do track you to that ruin, they're welcome to follow our wheel ruts along the old post road until they lose them amongst the older ones. Where we're turning off runs over nigh half a furlong of slickrock being washed even slicker by all this rain. Three

8

miles on is where we hole up until we get word it's safe to go on over the San Andres to Alamogordo."

Longarm never asked what was in the railroad town of Fat Cottonwoods, as Alamogordo translated. He figured he was supposed to know. It commenced to hail again, and although they were comfortable enough with a leather roof over them, they couldn't talk much, and the mules were driven half-loco. He could only hope they knew where they were going as they ran wildly through the blinding thunderation. Then they topped a rise too gentle to notice from any distance, and Longarm could make out not-too-distant lamplight ahead through the soggy shifting curtains.

They were met by shifty kid-sized shapes as they sloshed into the door yard of wherever this might be. When she said they were there, Longarm helped her down from the rig, and they ran for the door opening in welcome under the dripping ramada of what had to be a long sprawl of 'dobe ranch housing. They didn't look back, but took it on faith that the gnomes or whatever they were would see to the spent team and waterlogged rig.

Longarm's toes were squishing in his boots, and his tobacco-brown tweed smelled like a coon hound that could have used a bath. But he felt warmer if not drier as they were enveloped in the aromas of greasewood coals and those soapy-scented candles Mexican folks favored. More than one such candle burned in a nearby wall sconce. So Longarm was able to get his first good look at the mystery gal he'd ridden all that way with.

He managed to keep a poker face.

It wasn't easy.

There was no other way to put it.

Whatever else she might be, she was just plain beautiful.

Chapter 2

Seeing she was waiting and he had to say something, Longarm took the soggy wet sombrero off and tried. "They told me to expect a pretty face, but they never told me you were *this* pretty, *bonita*."

She blinked and demanded, "Bonita? My name is *Hazel*, Shadow! Didn't Sand tell you that?"

Longarm answered with an ease he didn't feel. "Sure, but I still think *bonita* fits you better. *No habla usted 'spañol?*"

She protested, "Do I look like a fool greaser? What might Bonita mean?"

He said, "Pretty. You look more like a play-pretty than a hazelnut to this child, but have it your way if you'd rather I call you Hazel."

She fluttered her lashes and replied, "I reckon I don't mind you calling me a play-pretty. Before we feed you we got to get you out of them wet duds, and I'd as soon change to something drier. Come with me."

He followed her through the rambling 'dobe rancho that should not have have been where it was, and she led him into a warm bathroom with English indoor plumbing.

It would have been dumb to ask where anyone in the trade of hiding riders on the Owlhoot Trail got the money for such up-to-date notions out in a poorly surveyed desert.

Still wearing her rain slicker, Hazel bent over to turn the hot water tap, muttering dark Gypsy threats in the unlikely event the greasers who worked there hadn't kept a fire under the boiler since the rain began.

As steam rose around them, she told him to shed his duds and get in, adding she'd send a hired hand to replace his wet tweeds and hickory shirt with a robe and his soggy boots with slippers. As soon as he was alone, Longarm hung his six-gun up, placed his soggy wallet and pocket contents on a handy tile shelf, and slipped his derringer into a nearby soap dish before he stripped and got in, hissing with unexpected pleasure when he realized how chilled to the bone he'd been.

Lathered up and soaking, Longarm proceeded to put together the very few pieces of the puzzle he had to work with so far.

Hazel's country accent rang of a girlhood in Bleeding, Kansas, just to the east of Colorado. The rail line running through the Alamogordo she'd mentioned fanned north from El Paso with the San Andres between it and the Denver & Rio Grande he'd been riding north with Clem Aherne. *That* line was a northern spur of the Southern Pacific, headed for—where else?—Kansas. A hardcase Kansas bad man who robbed banks and post offices was known as Sand, not the more common Sandy, Lachlan. Longarm hadn't worked the case, but things were commencing to fall into place as he went over the little he'd cared to know about the holdup man they'd picked up in El Paso, thanks to Victorio and the border crossing being closed during the current Apache scare.

Other lawmen had tried in vain to intercept a run for the border along the D&RG. Longarm saw now that the

11

owlhoots had streaked east to a more or less parallel rail line south to El Paso, where things had gone wrong. Clem Aherne had been picked up while they were stuck north of the border for the time being. So knowing Aherne knew too much and had his own neck to save with some singing, his gang had hired the late Shadow Manners, whoever he'd been, to make certain Aherne never imitated a canary bird in the First District Court of Colorado.

A shyly smiling old Mexican came in with a fluffy dry robe of white Turkish toweling and a pair of rope-soled sandals. He hung them up and left with Longarm's wet clothes, never saying a word. He likely spoke little English. Longarm had already regretted letting Hazel know he spoke some Spanish. He just didn't *know* whether Shadow Manners had spoken Spanish or not. It was safer to leave that up in the air by just not bragging.

He was only *guessing* Shadow Manners had been outside help the gang had recruited to do a job on their pal. Thinking back, Longarm realized that either Aherne had been mighty dumb about the intentions of a gang member he'd recognized, or he simply hadn't known Shadow on sight. The straw sombrero and the fact that he had to have gotten aboard in El Paso smacked of a border *buscadero* one could hire by the hour, but again, the less one bragged about things one just didn't know, the less chance there was of putting both feet in it.

Hence "Shadow Manners" seemed wrapped in silent thought as he joined Hazel in front of a cozy chaparral fire in the sitting room. She looked sort of wrapped in thought too, wearing a fluffy robe and sandals that matched his own. Women looked more naked than men gussied up in fluffy bathrobes with nothing under them as far as Longarm could tell.

The discreetly silent Mexican help that seemed to go with the place no matter who owned it had put a handsome spread of tamales, tortillas, and such, along with a pitcher of sangria, on a coffee table before the fire. As they sat on the floor like kids toasting marshmallows, Hazel said old Hernan had hung Longarm's wet clothes in the boiler room to dry. He said that sounded about right, riding with a mighty gentle hand on the reins.

As she poured two goblets of the red wine punch that only *looked* sort of bloody, as "sangria" translated, Hazel allowed that she wasn't expecting Skippy, whoever the hell *he* might be, that side of noon, if then. She said, "You know how Sand is. He'll probably wait to see what the newspapers have to say about the job you did on Clem before he sends us word one way or the other."

"Old Sand's sure cautious," Longarm agreed, adding, "But who are we to fault a mastermind too slick for the law by half?"

She washed down a mouthful of tapa before she replied. "You know it. Soon as the law snagged Clem, Sand had us spread out miles apart with orders to stay put until further orders. This spread belongs to some greasers who trade guns for horses with the Mescaleros on the far side of the San Andres. I don't know where they might be right now. Sand says it's best when folks can't peach on one another. But they were the ones who suggested you and I meet up at that abandoned stagecoach stop."

Longarm helped himself to a wad of tortilla as he observed, "Old Sand sure must like to play chess. In the dark. With the other side wearing blindfolds. I bet he never told you how much I was getting for the job or where he means to pay off, right?"

She said, "A lot you know! I may be just a girl, but I'll have you know I'm more than an errand girl. I know he gave you half your five up front, with the rest to be paid after he reads you nailed Clem and got away clean. Why are you gnawing that bone, Shadow? Don't you trust

13

Sand to keep his word to you once we all meet up again in Alamogordo?"

"The thought never crossed my mind," Longarm lied as he examined that new piece while sipping sangria a good ways off from the murderous gang leader.

Five hundred was the going price for an uncomplicated killing at the hands of a hired gun. Killing a hired gun could get complicated in its own right, and the savings to be gained by double-crossing the murderous Shadow Manners only amounted to $250.

On the other hand, Sand Lachlan hadn't hesitated to have a closer pal killed, while on the *other* hand, who was going to go up against a killer with Shadow Manners's rep for another five hundred or more?

Hazel asked what he was smiling to himself about. He told her truthfully, "Just considering how many wheels you can fit within wheels once you put your mind to it. The simple answer is usually the best answer, provided you know what the question is. Sometimes you don't. That's when you lie awake, staring at the ceiling, trying to fit the gears together."

She stared into the embers of the dying fire for a time before she murmured, "I know what you're trying to figure out, Shadow. I've been thinking in the same circles. I guess Sand told you about Frenchy and me, right?"

Longarm cautiously replied, "If he did, I wasn't paying much mind to such beeswax, no offense."

She murmured, "Frenchy won't get out for another year, if we're lucky, but I am his woman, and I love him like crazy, Shadow!"

Longarm said, "I follow your drift. Your Frenchy is a fortunate cuss, Miss Hazel."

She almost sobbed. "Call me Bonita. It doesn't sound as false to my Frenchy if you call me by a name he's never heard me called, see?"

Longarm took his time washing down more grub, and then, seeing he was expected to say something, he said, "You're going to have to spell things out a tad clearer . . . Bonita. I wouldn't want a pretty gal to consider me a sissy, but if another rider of the Owlhoot Trail has a claim on you . . ."

"He does. I love him, but he's been in prison for three years now, and I'm a natural woman with natural feelings who's not getting any younger as one lonely night follows yet another!"

Longarm started to take her in his arms. She stiffened and gasped, "Not out here where the greasers might catch us, Shadow. In my room, with the door barred and your word as a man not to ever tell a soul!"

He soberly assured her he just hated a kiss-and-tell. So she got to her feet first to lead him by the hand to her room with not a servant the wiser as far as they could tell.

As Hazel barred the door, Longarm took the palmed derringer from the robe's pocket to discreetly cache it between the mattress and bed rail as he sat on the mattress.

As she turned from barring the door, Hazel shot him a thoughtful look and decided, "I reckon you do have the right to feel sure of yourself. I reckon you have me down in your book as an awful slut, right?"

"Not hardly," he lied, knowing he was damned if he did and damned if he didn't. It was possible she was putting him to a test. Lots of gals on the wrong side of the law had heard no lawman could arrest a gal he'd had his wicked way with. Lots of gals on the wrong side of the law had been chagrined to learn that like many a pool-hall notion about women, that wasn't exactly the way things worked.

A lawman wasn't *supposed* to "compromise himself" with anybody he was likely to haul into court. That was what they called fucking a felon or a material witness, compromising. But on the other hand, half the gals who'd ever been hauled in had accused the arresting officers of rape, so things tended to even out.

Male suspects were forever winding up in jail by trusting too much in that other old saw about a wife not being allowed to testify against her husband. That wasn't the way that one read. She couldn't be forced against her will to put her man in jail. But as many a man had found out, she had the right to testify against *anybody* to keep her *own* ass out of jail. So Longarm made a mental note about that as Hazel joined him on the bed and he forgot all about legal technicalities for a spell.

Once all that Turkish toweling fell out of the way as if by magic, he found it easier to believe she hadn't had any for years. She was all over him with a ferocity that made him glad she was such a tiny little thing. Then he was in her with her on top, and had she been tinier *that* way it never would have gone in.

"Oh, my lands!" she marveled. "Nobody ever told me these things could come so big!" And so it wasn't long before she was coming, with him coming close behind, and she liked it even better, she purred, with him on top.

He was just as glad that, having mentioned her locked-up Frenchy by way of invitation, she was smart enough to leave the cuss in prison and say no more about him. One of the things that kept Longarm off married women as much as or more than the Good Book was the habit so many of them had in bed of gloating about the way they were pulling the wool over the eyes of a brute who didn't deserve them. Some men likely got a boot out of hanging horns on a poor simp who'd never done 'em wrong. But the few times he'd done it, Longarm had felt sort of dirty. Any sneak could steal change off a blind newsdealer or fuck another man's woman behind his back.

Having held on to the pocket contents of his wet duds, Longarm groped for the robe he'd dropped on the rug to produce a damp three-for-a-nickel cheroot and fortunately waterproof Mexican matches for a second-wind smoke with the two of them propped against the headboard.

Hazel marveled at the Mexican matches. He'd been right about her and the gang being based in Kansas, he could see, as he explained how they made that brand down Mexico way by dipping the heads as well as the stems in a hard white wax they got from some tree they grew down yonder. The pasteboard box they came in was waterproofed with wax as well.

As he got their cheroot going, Hazel said, "Sand said you were a Texican border jumping man with . . . moo hairs on both sides of the Rio Grande. Do I screw as hot as a Mex moo hair?"

He chuckled and said, "The word you're groping for is *mujer,* and if you screwed any nicer, it could be injurious to a man's health. I don't like to talk about women who ain't present when I'm in bed with another, Bonita."

She snuggled closer and said she felt safer about their own arrangement. He smiled with the cheroot gripped in his teeth and asked if she meant the others were to take them for no more than business associates once the gang was all there.

She said, "Oh, land's sakes, I've been fending the boys off since my Frenchy was arrested by saying I'd promised to be true."

He didn't answer.

She said, "I meant what I was saying too! I'm still trying to fathom what came over me tonight when our eyes first met by candlelight. I know you think I'm lying, but I wasn't planning on nothing like this when my knees went weak and I was suddenly all wet betwixt my thighs!"

He put the smoke to her lips as he said soothingly, "The feeling was mutual. I suspect we started out wetter and more excited than usual. That Professor Darwin over in the Old Country thinks we're all evolved from folk inclined to feel reproductive in times of peril. That's likely why war and rape seem to go together, and any war vet can tell you how much wilder women acted when they saw the men were in uniform."

He mentally kicked his own bare ass as he realized he'd talked too much. He didn't know whether the late Shadow Manners had served with old Hood's Brigade, some Confederate guerrillas such as Sibley's West Texas Raiders, or for all Longarm knew, seeing Manners had been tied in with Kansas riders, the *Union*. Old Sam Houston had sided with the Union, and you didn't get more Texican than *him*!

But from the way Hazel cuddled and spooned, he hadn't put his foot in it yet. So he encouraged her to do most of the talking, leading her some as an experienced questioner until, before it came time to try it doggy-style, he'd established that she and her Kansas pals were indeed under the leadership of the notorious Sand Lachlan of Ford County, wanted in Dodge for the cold-blooded murder of yet another business associate.

Hazel seemed to think the double-crosser had had it coming. She added that as soon as Sand thought the coast was clear, they'd all be gathering at Alamogordo to settle accounts, with everybody getting what Sand felt he or she deserved.

18

Chapter 3

It rained fire and salt all night to resettle the caliche or desert pavement as smooth as tablecloth betwixt washes and clumps of chaparral or *tuna* as the local Mexicans called prickly pear. As the rain smoothed the caliche, dried-out alkali salts would mortar the birdcage-sized gravel to re-form a brittle gray crust that would hold foot, hoof, or wagon tracks until the next good rain. Trackers who trusted in this were inclined to think no tracks across the caliche ahead meant nobody had ever crossed it. The cemented-together gravel had been sorted to be suitable for birdcages by the drier winds that carried off finer grit as lost-forever dust or distant sand dunes in the lee of higher rises. The alkali salts were the curse of all arid lands where rare rainwater tended to stay put and suck anything soluble to the surface as it baked in the sun.

With any luck, the body of the real Shadow Manners should have wound up in one of the lower *playas* or temporary desert lakes, hopefully well covered with its own crust of floodwater mud and thus invisible from a distance.

Nobody with a lick of sense rode out across a *playa*

where a thin crust of eggshell dry mud could be covering deep alkaline slime months after the last flooding. But if somebody found him, how easy might he be to recognize by the time they did?

Knowing better than to trust a woman whose man in prison couldn't trust *her,* Longarm had hidden his badge and personal papers in the lining of his dried-out coat of tobacco tweed, using a slit he'd had a tailor line and hem for him back in Denver with just such emergencies in mind. So he felt it safe to leave his wallet with just the cash on hand and no identification where his "Bonita" or perhaps a nosy house servant could get at it.

Even though he knew it was safe to speak Spanish in front of a gal who had him down as a border *buscadero,* Longarm went easy with it in front of the hired help. They seemed to speak enough English to serve their guests, and Longarm knew he was known on both sides of the border, a lot, as an involuntary hero of La Revolución known as El Brazo Largo as *Longarm* came out in Border Mexican.

The current dictatorship of El Presidente Diaz having a few admirers as well as a heap of dissatisfied customers, Mexican folks that far south were forever trying get him killed or fix him up with a sister. So it was a lot safer to be taken for another yanqui chingado they'd been ordered to feed and shelter by a person or persons Hazel wasn't too clear about.

She said Sand Lachlan had lots of connections along the Owlhoot Trail.

By the time they'd spent close to forty-eight hours there, since nobody could spend all that time screwing, the two of them had explored the layout well enough to decide their unknown host or hosts had to be invisible or, more likely, up or down the tracks in, say, Engel or Rincon, where the D&RG parted company with the Rio Grande for its shortcut across the Jornado del Muerto. In either case, not to be found at home by any posse that might drop by.

How were they supposed to know the hired killer they were hiding from the law was a lawman who'd already taken bearings on two distant peaks from their unmapped way station along the Owlhoot Trail?

Both those high, distant peaks of the San Andres *would* be on the map, and where the bearing Longarm had taken crossed, out in the middle of hitherto blank paper, would give the location of this one hideout.

That still left other hideouts. Every time he brought the topic up, Hazel said they had to wait there for Skippy Steiner and suggested they lie down somewhere to talk about how they'd keep Skippy from guessing what they'd been up to.

Hazel did that swell. But as enjoyable as the petite Kansas brunette was, Longarm was eager to go on, and by the time you'd had three nights and many a stolen daytime tussle with the same gal, it tended to become a *chore,* even when you had nothing else on your mind.

Longarm had told more than one wistful gal, and partly meant it, that he was still single because no man who toted a badge and lived by the gun had any right to saddle such a pretty little thing with premature widowhood. He'd been to enough funerals to tell himself he was sincere about that point. But falling head over heels and having to move on in a day or so had its points as well. It was a caution how, no matter how gals started out with a man, they all set out to change his ways and plan his future by the time they'd gotten him to talking mushy.

Some kindly old philosopher had once written, no doubt in French, that since men all wanted the girl of their dreams to stay just the same as she was when they met, while all women hoped to change every man they met to the man of their dreams, both were doomed to disappointment.

Hazel had for chrissake been waiting by the tracks in the rain for a hardcase hired gun with bad Mexican habits. Yet even as she said she was waiting for another infernal outlaw to get out of prison and make a dishonest woman of her, she'd taken to chiding Longarm about sucking on a durned cheroot when she had two whole tits to offer, and hinting about maybe leaving old Frenchy to find another gal if Longarm wanted to take her south of the border and teach her some Spanish to go with her French kissing.

So Longarm, at least, was mighty pleased to meet up with Skippy Steiner when the skinny young shit finally showed up on a paint barb, leading a pair of buckskin scrubs. Hazel had already let it slip that Skippy and the late Shadow Manners hadn't met up yet.

As the three of them dined outdoors at a trestle table set up in the shade of a cactus-rib ramada, Skippy brought them up to date on things.

He said Sand was calling everyone in to settle accounts at a *posada* near the railroad stop in Alamogordo, pleased as punch about the way the papers had agreed on the shooting aboard that D&RG night flyer.

The *Rocky Mountain News,* covering more details with the help of their stringer with a day job on the railroad, had reported how some unknown assailant remembered mostly for his big sombrero had shot that federal prisoner handcuffed to the famous Longarm bold as brass.

Skippy said, "Papers say Longarm uncuffed hisself from Clem and lit out after you. So now they're worried about *him.* The conductor didn't know a lawman had jumped off after what he took for just your murderous self. So he signaled the engineer to get 'em on up to the telegraph at Engel. Old Sand's worried about Longarm

22

too. Might the two of you have shot it out in the desert?"

Longarm truthfully replied, "I did peg a shot at an unfriendly muzzle flash amid all that wind, rain, and hail. Can't say whether I hit anybody for certain. *Hope* I did!"

Skippy said, "So does Sand. Longarm's pals ain't the only ones worried about him. They say he's one hell of a tracker as well as nobody to mess with. Sand would have sent me sooner if he hadn't been brooding about a tracker with one hell of a rep on your tail."

Hazel said, "We've been waiting here for days, Skippy. Shadow must have killed him too. Where might this famous Longarm be if he's still alive?"

The skinny youth with an old man's eyes said, "That's how Sand reads her. Whether he lost your trail or not, he'd have surely headed back to the tracks the first dry day out here. He wasn't packing canteens or other desert gear. They say he even left his *hat* aboard that train. How long would a man last with no hat and no water on the Jornado del Muerto? He must be *down* somewhere out yonder. Dead by this time, whether Shadow hit him or not. Papers say they've scouted in vain for bodies. Sand says there's too much wide-open space out yonder to make it worth their while. This rancho's been here for years and nobody's scouted her yet, have they?"

Longarm asked how Skippy had ever found his way there across all that wide-open space.

Skippy replied, "Didn't Sand tell you? Him, me, Winks Malloy, and old Clem Aherne hid out here a month summer before last. That's how come he sent me to fetch you both. We're to leave after sundown when it's cooler riding and nobody on a far-off mesa with a telly-scope can pick you out as you top a rise."

Longarm, seeing he was supposed to be the one who'd murdered Skippy's former sidekick Clem Aherne, knew better than to ask how Skippy felt about such draconian

23

measures on the part of an all-knowing and all-wise Sand Lachlan. He asked in a mild tone how the three of them were supposed to make it far as Alamogordo on those swell cow ponies out back. Longarm said, "I'm sure you know this country better. But it seems to me we are talking about fifteen or twenty miles to the craggy-as-crumpled-paper and dry-as-mummy-wrappings San Andres. After which we have to cross another thirty miles or more of the Tularosa Valley, which, last time I looked, was nigh as dry everywhere but that twenty miles or more of crushed blackboard chalk they call the White Sands Desert."

Skippy easily replied, "We'll be swinging north around the White Sands. We'll be changing mounts along the way. You didn't think I rid all this way from Alamogordo with them three sorry nags, did you?"

Longarm managed not to say the thought had occurred to him. The skinny kid with an old man's eyes had just handed him another secret of the Owlhoot Trail. Like a coach line, the rascals had relay stations out in the middle of the unmapped nowhere at handy intervals.

Longarm had his own secrets when it came to questioning suspects. He never put them on guard by asking more questions than he really needed to. Thanks to all those pillow conversations with the love-starved Hazel, he already knew she'd dropped off a slow freight out of Rincon like a hobo, and been picked up in the desert by that surrey that worked out of this hideout he'd already located. On another occasion, doggy-style, the excited little thing had confided that she could hardly wait to get him back up to the bright lights and Don't Disturb signs of wicked Wichita. He'd established without asking, old-fashioned-style, that the gang had relocated there after they'd been run out of Dodge. She'd bragged, on top, about how they'd used Wichita as a safe neck of the

24

woods between jobs, with Sand and the boys never hitting
a bank within a hard day's ride and staying spread out in
the big city, rooming in different boardinghouses, wining
and dining in different joints and, as she'd observed with
a wicked grin, screwing in different parts of town.

So the question before the house was where the gang
hid out as they ranged out from Wichita. Rounding up
some of them or even all of them where they'd never
robbed anybody would be a feather in any lawman's cap,
but nothing to mapping out and breaking up a good-sized
stretch of the Owlhoot Trail.

Longarm was too realistic to hope for more than a pro-
tem crimp in what was more a state of mind than an ever-
shifting network of hideouts with new faces replacing
those hiding out as fast as they could be rounded up.

Longarm knew full well that other lawmen would be
tracking other riders of the Owlhoot Trail long after he
was gone. But looking on the bright side, he was never
going to run out of work as long as he lived.

After they'd eaten, following the customs of their un-
seen Mexican hosts and the servants hired by them, the
three Anglos agreed to meet up for more planning and
sangria after *la siesta* ended, around four in the afternoon
or later, depending on the sun now glaring down from a
cloudless cobalt sky with all the moisture of that recent
summer storm sucked out of the parched caliche.

Longarm and Hazel had agreed before Skippy joined
them that their secret affair would have to lie hidden until
they got up to that place in wicked Wichita nobody but
she and the incarcerated Frenchy knew of.

But once Longarm was spread out naked in the chamber assigned to him, his Bonita had shown up in that fluffy
robe to confide with a giggle that Skippy was tucked away
with one of the house servants and a pitcher of *pulque,*
which was stronger, if less sweet, than sangria.

When Longarm asked whether Skippy was in bed with a she-servant or a he-servant, she said her Shadow was just awful. When she asked how he'd known about Skippy, Longarm replied, "Lucky guess," but being a woman, she kept at him about it until he explained, doggy-style, "Your boss, Sand, seems to favor wispy side-kicks who keep their girlish figures as their eyes grow ever older. Clem Aherne had that same prison-punk look before Sand decided he'd be better off dead. He likely feared an ex-con who'd do anything to stay on the good side of stronger men would be likely to do anything to stay on the good side of the stronger men who'd arrested him."

Hazel arched her spine to take him deeper as she decided, "I know you've spent your own share of hard time behind bars, you randy thing. Did you ever, you know, treat other boys in prison this naughty?"

He thrust teasingly and answered, truthfully enough when you studied on it, "No way I could have. I've never been locked up with any other boys hung nice as you, *bonita mia.*"

She laughed like hell, and by the time they'd finished the old-fashioned way, she'd let it slip that Sand Lachlan in point of fact liked to shove it the same way to girls as well as boys. She added, "That's how I found it so easy to stay true to Frenchy, most of the time. The one time Sand asked, I was able to keep him out of my bung by weeping and wailing about never queering anybody but my one true love. I suspect Sand respects my Frenchy more than most. My Frenchy is really Scotch-Irish, but he killed a bigger man in Coffeeville with his feet one time."

Longarm got more gossip about the gang out of her as she got what she wanted out of him. At supper time, along about sundown in the Spanish way, Skippy looked as if he'd enjoyed his siesta as well. Then it was as dark as

Skippy wanted it and the three of them rode out, the two men astride on Mexican roping saddles with wooden swells while Hazel rode sidesaddle of course. Skippy had brought along a Winchester Yellowboy as his own saddle gun and provided his pal Shadow Manners with an even older Spencer. They each packed two canteens of water without bedrolls or trail grub. Skippy explained they only had to make it far as the not-too-far San Andres Mountains, if one wanted to call a glorified windrow of dusty rubble mountains.

So they rode, and rode some more, breaking once an hour and using up half their water by the time the full moon was rising behind the black ridges ahead to paint the caliche silver between darker patches of chaparral. So they could see things fairly clearly for about a furlong ahead, and when that staggered line of other riders loomed ever closer in the moonlight, it was Hazel who gasped, "I sure hope somebody tells me I'm wrong! For I could swear all those riders ahead with white stripes across their dark faces look like *Indians*!"

Longarm put a casual hand to the butt of his borrowed Spencer as he quietly replied, "You ain't wrong, Miss Hazel. They look like Mescaleros."

Hazel gasped, *"Mescaleros?* Surely you don't mean Mescalero *Apache*!"

To which he could only reply, "There ain't no other kind of Mescalero."

Chapter 4

Skippy said, "Hesh up and let me do the talking," before he called out, "That you, Rosario? How come you boys are wearing paint tonight? You look like Victorio's bronco bunch!"

A deeper voice in fair English salted with Mission Spanish called out, "We don't want the blue sleeves from Fort Stanton to know any other sort of Na-dene are off that fucking reservation. The blue sleeves have a big spyglass and a winking sun-box up on Pico Salinas. The talking wire has them looking for somebody out on these *baldios*. Better they should take us for *los broncos* than *escaparsos*, eh? Come, you have ridden slow and is better nobody sees anybody with that *chingado* spyglass, eh?"

So everybody was soon moving west toward the looming blackness of the low but rugged San Andres Mountains at an uncomfortable but mile-eating trot. Hazel bitched about the gait because you couldn't stand in the stirrups worth mention in a sidesaddle. So she got a good spanking as they trotted quite a spell.

As they did so, the moon seemed to be moving backward in the sky above until it appeared to have set behind the ink-black jagged peaks looming up ahead, and the three whites could only hope their Indian guides knew what they were up to as they rode on and on through pitch darkness all around.

Longarm could see enough skyline on either side to sense they'd ridden up a canyon, and the trail he could only trust his buckskin to follow had many a kink to offer before they rounded a bend to ride into the soft amber glow of little night fires all around. Then he could see they'd made it to the *rancheria* of Rosario's band, wherever in hell it was and who in blue blazes Rosario might be.

Most Indian children, since they were almost never punished, tended to be well-behaved, and most Indian dogs, since they were often eaten, had little tendency to bark. So the entry of the riders stirred up less of a fuss than riding into a more civilized-looking settlement might have.

Mescaleros living on the move as they had in their Shining Times were inclined to dwell in wickiups that resembled Eskimo igloos improvised from brush, or the upside-down nests of fair-sized robin. But as Longarm got his bearings to either side of the pony track up the steep-walled canyon, he saw that this particular Mescalero band had settled in to stay a spell in more substantial Mexican jacales of more serious construction, or in some cases 'dobe *casitas* a casual eye just passing through could mistake for the abodes of poor but honest Mexicans.

Longarm figured that was the general idea as he regarded the impassive folks watching from windows and doorways to either side. For only the bare-legged and painted Indians riding in with the whites looked all that Indian. A lot of the local gals and some of the men were dressed as if to go to Mass in a mission town closer to the Pecos or the Rio Grande. Take your pick. Longarm was used to the ways of the so-called Pueblo or Village Indians blending with those of their Hispanic neighbors. But he'd never noticed folks described by the B.I.A. and War Department as "Apache" settled down as much as Rosario's band.

They perforce rode in column up the narrow canyon trail, with Rosario and Skippy chatting in the lead, so Longarm and Hazel could hear the soft laconic comments from either side without understanding most of them. Some were in Spanish, and it was just as well the perky brunette riding sidesaddle didn't speak that lingo. Remarks in Na-dene, the far more difficult lingo shared by the so-called Apache and their Navajo cousins, were likely as disrespectful.

Hearing Spanish in a Mescalero *rancheria* wasn't all that unusual. You had to be born and raised on Na-dene to wrap your tongue around it with any comfort. Longarm could make himself understood in some of the far easier Indian tongues, but according to more than one linguist Longarm had talked to, the dialects of Na-dene shared by the so-called Apache, Navajo, and original Dene reindeer hunters of Siberia and northern Canada, still up there and bothering nobody, was one of the most complicated lingos ever devised by the mind of man.

A white man and, say, a Lakota or a Cheyenne could agree a critter was a *dog,* a *shunka,* or a *mita.* If you asked a Na-dene speaker how he might say "dog," he would ask you whether you meant a dog that was present, a dog that was out of sight, a dog that was running, sitting still, or maybe dead.

So not even other Indians messed with learning Na-dene, and since all the nations in the Southwest had been exposed to Mission Spanish and Mexican Trade jargon, they spoke Spanish to Na-dene and vice versa. The resulting Spanish influence on them had resulted in many

30

of them winding up with Spanish names, from Cochise to Victorio, or in this case Rosario. So all those snotty Spanish remarks that evening could be coming from visitors from other nations. More than one usually expected in your average unregulated *rancheria*.

They wound up milling in the dooryard of a more substantial 'dobe that a lot of Mexicans would have been proud to live in. Indian kids without that war paint offered help with the horses, and one helped Hazel down with a smile as he told her in Spanish what he'd like to do to her if only she were a captive instead of an honored guest. Longarm took charge of her with as charming a smile, murmuring, *"No le busques cinco patas al gato, muchacho!"*

The sassy kid surrendered Hazel's arm with a grin and: *"Pero lamento porque se que nunca voy a joder una gringa."*

As he led Hazel on, Longarm muttered, "That was no Indian. His Spanish was better than mine."

Hazel asked what she'd missed. Longarm said, "I suggested it was dumb to look for five paws on a cat, or needless trouble."

Then, since, what the hell, they knew each other in the Biblical sense, doggy-style, he confided, "He allowed how sad he felt because now he was never going to fuck a gringo gal. Mescaleros call us White Eyes. Gringo, or in your case *gringa*, is a pure Mexican endearment. I thought some of this crowd had to be Mexican. Minds me of those Metís settlements up Canada way. Disgruntled breeds and full-bloods gathered in mutual opposition to the powers that be. This settlement can't be operating with the approval of the Bureau of Indian Affairs and the Army can't know it's here. But they don't seem to be on the warpath. So, like Miss Alice said, this is sure getting curiouser and curiouser."

They were led inside Rosario's rambling 'dobe *casa*. Most of the Indians, or whatever they were, stayed outside. Rosario, a few of his lieutenants, and the three whites got to sit on Navajo rugs carpeting the dirt floor as shy Mescalero gals served bowls of pony, blue corn, and piñyon nut stew all around. Longarm had been too keyed-up to keep track of the last time he'd eaten. But as he dug in with a rolled-up tortilla, combining the features of of fork, spoon, and bread, he realized it had been more than six hours since they'd had supper at that other way station along the Owlhoot Trail.

Rosario, once one of his wives or daughters had wiped that white war paint away for him with a wet towel, turned out to be a ruggedly handsome man in his forties, charming as most of his breed when they weren't fixing to kill you.

Longarm had expected nothing less from an authority figure raised to a warrior code. He'd learned in his teens, during that war they'd held in his honor, how farm-boy recruits brawled and cussed way more than old soldiers, who followed stiff rules of military courtesy when parleying with the enemy. Men more inclined to shoot or stab than to punch or kick were more inclined to smile and address a stranger as "sir" while they made up their minds. When you fought to the death, you didn't start fights as lightly as Saturday night drunks.

Playing dumb, seated closer to Hazel, Longarm just listened as Skippy and their Mescalero host did most of the talking. Rosario said he would send them on their way with fresh mounts come morning. Skippy allowed he'd feel safer along the mountain trails the next night, seeing the Army had that long-range telescope up on Salinas Peak to the north.

Rosario shook his head and said, "When two paths seem dangerous, it is best to take the least dangerous path, little brother. Pico Salinas is far, far to the north. So the blue sleeves cannot see behind the closer peaks or down into the passes and canyons with the strongest spyglass from that vantage point."

Skippy said, "They only have to glimpse movement once before they heliograph our position in every blamed direction, Chief! They're all riled up about a famous lawman Shadow yonder dropped on the desert for them to look for. Lawmen and soldiers blue are stirred up like red ants out of a stomped-on nest. I'll feel way safer crossing over the divide in the dark."

The Indian who lived in those parts said, "You may *feel* safer, little brother. A deer that feels safe is easier to hit with your arrow. I know you people do not believe in the *chindi* who haunt the trails after dark to trap real people. But the trails themselves are treacherous, very treacherous. In many places very narrow as they cling to the sides of cliffs. Hear me. You will be better off taking your chances with that far-off observation post!"

Skippy said, "We're already running late. I don't want to risk our pals in Alamogordo leaving without us. I'll allow we've had about enough night riding for now. But do we rest up here until, say, three o'clock in the morning, we ought to be way up in those craggy passes you bragged on by sunrise, and do we day-camp in a canyon and ride down the far slope and out across the Tularosa flats under cover of darkness . . ."

"You are going to get yourself and a good mule killed!" Rosario finished.

But Skippy was insistent, and it appeared from odd scraps Longarm was able to put together that Rosario took orders from the unknown Mexicans who ran that way station closer to the tracks. So Longarm was working on how come when the older man gave in with: "*Bueno*, I have been told that pretty woman with you is the *mujer* of a

33

comrade in prison. So I shall put a guard by the door of her guest room. Do you *hombres* wish for to lie down together or in separate rooms?"

Skippy flushed red and said, "That gossip about me and Sand ain't true! I like women just as much as you do, Chief!"

Rosario chuckled dryly and asked, "Who said I liked women? The three of you will be shown to your rooms now. If you really mean to make it up among the crags by sunrise, you will have to be on your way before three. I don't see how you'll catnap long enough to matter, but Don Carillo says your wish must be our command, and if you fall off a cliff in your sleep, do not say I did not warn you!"

Then Rosario rattled orders in his own difficult lingo, and a Mescalero gal was leading Longarm somewhere with a rush light in her free hand.

He didn't get a good look at her until she'd led him into an 'dobe walled chamber with a solid wooden door and two rifle slits by way of ventilation. She wasn't delicate-featured enough to describe as pretty. Her big pale amber eyes staring out above high cheekbones were about as nice to look at as the eyes of, say, a friendly mountain lioness.

Waving the rush light at the sleeping pallet against one wall, she told him in Spanish she was called Carlita and she'd been ordered to keep track of the time and wake him up in two hours.

She demurely added, "I have found, when following the men on a raid, it hurts more to wake up from no more than an hour's sleep than it does to just go on, tired or not."

Longarm said he'd noticed the same thing, scouting Indians for the blue sleeves. Mescaleros had courtly manners but respected honest enemies.

Carlita laughed softly and said, "We do not have for to play that game. Rosario has not fought your kind since Redbeard made peace with Cochise and our Chiricahua cousins. I am a, how you say, *friendly* Indian!"

He asked her how friendly as he played for time, not wanting to clam her up by asking point-blank what her band was doing out this way if they weren't living bronco.

Carlita shut and barred the door as she replied, "Friendly enough for to help you pass an hour more pleasantly than trying half the time for to fall asleep and then cursing me for waking you up as soon as you manage perhaps."

He saw she thought the Spanish phrase *tal vez* translated into her own lingo as "Strip!" for there was no *tal vez* or *perhaps* in the way she shucked her one-piece cotton smock over her head and marched over to the bedding in her shin-high Mescalero moccasins.

Longarm had met up with friendly Indians before. So he knew why she hunkered on the bedding but didn't lie down. They said *East* Indians fucked the same way, with the gal squatting on top.

As Longarm stripped, he reflected on dumb arguments about that sort of loving with other white men. Indian men, east or west, weren't being lazy when they lay flat on their backs and took their beatings like the considerate men they were shooting for. Indians east or west slept on the ground or, at most, thin matting such as that against the wall. So a gal's delicate tailbones could wind up bruised or worse after a spell of serious passion.

Carlita gasped, then giggled as Longarm lay bare-ass on the pallet and she saw what she was getting into her. But she was sport enough to play the game she'd started, and after some gingerly opening moves she was opened wide enough, and it sure beat all how fast folks could

35

come in that position if the gal's legs were strong enough to match her passion.

So they still had plenty of time for talk, and by the time she told him it was time to wake up, Longarm had another way station along the Owlhoot Trail located and explained in the mental notes he'd been making.

Rosario was neither a self-destructive bronco Apache like Victorio, nor a teacher's pet like the late Cochise. Knowing better than to buck the White Eyes head-on, and not wanting to live on handouts from the B.I.A., Rosario and his mixed band of full-bloods and free-thinking Mexican mestizos were in business for themselves, trading stolen stock and other loot to the gun-running Don Carillo for the guns and ammunition they gave wilder Indians for all they could steal from anybody. As they shared a smoke, Longarm managed not to chide Carlita for bragging by reflecting on how many pure Anglo-Saxons traded for stolen stock with firewater and worse while looking down their noses at greasers and redskins. He felt sort of shitty as he considered how the B.I.A. and War Department were going to deal with his official report, if ever he got out of this alive.

But you could only eat an apple a bite at a time or keep on living as you played your next moves by ear. So even though Carlita wistfully said she could use another good poking, Longarm had to ride on with Skippy and Hazel while he still had a hard-on, and he sure could have used some sleep.

Chapter 5

Rosario had mounted them on surefooted Spanish saddle mules, and he'd assigned two youths to guide them by moonlight and a single pony track one could only stray from by falling off a mountain. It took less than an hour to reach a moonlit swale, where one of their guides pointed at the silvery track through close-grazed grama and said, "That is the trail to the white sands. I don't think the three of you will get that far. If you meet anyone on the trail ahead, shoot them. They will be *chindi*, pretending to be real people wandering the hills like coyotes this late at night. Do not take time to see if their feet are on backward. Shoot them. Any real people pretending to be *chindi* deserve to die."

Since the conversation had been held in Spanish, Hazel had no idea what the problem was. She said she was having problems of her own. She said she hadn't caught five winks of sleep and felt insecure riding sidesaddle in the dark.

He told her to forget all she might have heard about the way ladies of fashion rode, and added, "It ain't a mortal sin to grab hold of that forward rest your pretty right knee is cocked over with your free hand, and if you feel surer with the reins in your right hand, go on and shift. The mule don't care and won't tell on you!"

She did just as he suggested, holding the reins in her right hand as she braced herself holding on with her left hand just over her right knee. She said it made her feel less likely to slide off the left side of her swaying mount as they rode on, then on some more, until they were moving up a moonless canyon and couldn't see shit.

When she bitched about that, Longarm said, "Come on, Miss Hazel. You druv that surrey through wind and rain as dark or darker the other night."

She protested, "That was then. Now I'm not seated squarely on a horizonal seat with my feet braced wide apart against the dashboard! Every step this big mule takes makes my derriere slip and slide on this slick leather incline!"

He said, "Hang on, trust your mount's night eyes, and if all else fails try to fall on the high side of the trail!"

She murmured murderously, "Very funny. How does a girl tell which side the high side might be when she can't see her hand before her face?"

Longarm said soothingly, "Skippy's mule, ahead of yours, is likely to step off a cliff first. Just don't follow them over the edge and you ought to be all right, Miss Hazel."

She didn't answer. She sounded as if she might be crying. Longarm didn't blame her. But boys weren't allowed to cry just because they were scared shitless, and if they turned back and let Skippy go on without them, there'd be nobody waiting when they finally made it to the railroad stop at Alamogordo.

They rode on and ever higher through passes wide and narrow, through some moonlight and far more shadow, until even surrounded by blackness they could see the sky above pearling lighter.

As the trail led out of a pass along a cliffside ledge by the dawn's early light, Skippy called back, "We'd best day-camp here, with that high rise to our north!"

Longarm was less worried about Army telescopes dozens of miles off in any kind of light than he was having some damned light on that treacherous footing ahead. He called ahead, "Nobody can see yonder ledge from the north, and I purely don't intend to move along *on foot* in the *dark*!"

Hazel sobbed that she didn't want to follow that ledge day or night, adding, "My poor feet will be hanging out over that abyss in this infernal sidesaddle, and what if my rump should slip?"

Skippy decided, "All right then. We'll ride on across by morning light and hole up on the far side."

So that's the way they tried her. The ledge got no wider as they had to follow it around blind turns with sheer rock to their right and that ass-puckering drop to their left. Swinging around an outside curve, Hazel yelled, "Oh, my land! I just looked down and wet myself!"

"Don't look down no more!" Longarm warned her as, up ahead, he heard Skippy calling, "We made it! I'm in another canyon now!"

But Hazel wasn't. They'd never know for certain, but maybe her mule stumbled under her, maybe pissing herself had made her saddle slicker, or maybe she'd just gone dizzy in her head, but all of a sudden her saddle was empty and she only managed one sad wail, like a locomotive whistle fading away in the night, as she bounced down the sheer cliff in the night in a series of dull wet thuds!

Her spooked mule carried her empty saddle out of sight at a lope that would have scared her to death if she'd still

39

been alive. Longarm didn't try to rein his own mount in as it tore after its remuda-mate, scaring the hell out of the already shaken Longarm. As they joined Skippy and the first two mules on wider and more solid footing, Skippy was holding Hazel's eye-rolling mule by the rein he'd managed to grab. Skippy gasped, "What happened? Where's Hazel?"

Longarm rode past, reined in, and dismounted as he tersely replied, "She fell off. Let's tether up and have a look!"

They did, securing all three mules to trailside scrub before they edged back to the awesome drop-off. The cleft Hazel had fallen into, widening ever more to the west, was more a giant fracture than an eroded canyon through rock faulted most every which way, but with most of the strata sloping higher to the east along the stretch they'd been crossing. So there was no streambed at the distant bottom of Hazel's screaming drop. The facing rock walls just got closer together to form a jagged-ass black crack, and that was all there was to be seen down yonder.

Skippy marveled, "Frenchy sure ain't going to like this! But I don't see how we'll ever recover her body now. Do you?"

Longarm said, "Knew an Army man who fell into a crack something like this one. One of his boots with the foot still in it finally washed out of a spring miles away. What's left of Miss Hazel ain't going nowheres till it rains some more." Then, since living women had been known to fib, he asked, "Who's Frenchy?"

Skippy sighed and said, "Her man. Set to get out of prison any day now and, like I said, he ain't going to like this. Killed a man back in Great Bend just for asking her to dance. You're my witness we were riding at a walk by daylight when the poor gal just fell off, right?"

Longarm said soothingly, "Your back was turned to

her and you were rounding a bend when it all happened too sudden for me to keep track, Skippy. So we might as well push on."

Skippy shot an edgy glance at the cloudless sky above before he replied, "It's broad-ass daytime, Shadow!"

Longarm said, "I noticed. And we're up among the eagle crags where nobody a mile away can draw a bead on us, but clefts just as deep and sudden are set for us like bear traps. I vote we work our way over the crest and down the far slope to a stretch where things flatten out enough for a cuss a pistol shot away to worry us."

As Skippy hesitated, Longarm added, "These mules could do with some mountain grama, mayhaps by a water hole, and we could both do with forty winks whilst they graze."

He waved the big sombrero at the nearest mule and added, "We're packing no bedrolls. Even as tired as we are, sleeping on dusty gravel ain't my style. Why don't we see if we can scout up a green canyon and drop off till we're too hungry to go on sleeping?"

"I should have asked those fucking Indians for some trail grub," the youth with an old man's eyes muttered.

Longarm couldn't resist saying, "I asked a fucking Indian back there. But she said they had no canned goods, and a gunny of parched corn didn't sound as tempting then as it does right now. Mescalero ain't big on trail grub. They say their young men fight better when they're hungry, and don't die as soon when they're gut-shot with empty bellies. Want me to take the lead for a spell?"

Skippy grumbled that Sand had put him in charge. Longarm didn't argue with the simple logic of that claim. Rosario had told them to leave the three valuable mules with a certain Mexican on the outskirts of Alamogordo. Longarm volunteered to lead Hazel's mount on.

So they mounted up to ride and ride some more until,

not long before noon, they found themselves in one of those tiny Garden of Edens desert lands are famous for.

As they tethered the mules to cottonwood saplings near a trickle of springwater through juicy sedge, Skippy marveled how the critters could browse leaves, graze sedge, or sip cool clean water as the spirit moved them. Longarm was too polite to say he'd already noticed that before he'd suggested they day-camp there.

Dumping out the stagnant water in their canteens to refill with springwater, the two of them moved up the slope through cottonwood shade to where the grass was still springy but dry down to the roots. As they flopped down side by side, Skippy said, "This is the life. I'm glad I listened to you, Shadow! How did you ever knew we'd come to such a swell place to hole up for the day?"

"You always do in lands of little rain. They call a dell like this an *oasis*. The shit growing so thick all around evolved, like that English professor said, to get by on way less water. So when it finds itself with plenty of water under cloudless sunny skies with nothing important browsing it back, you get what you see right now."

Longarm fished out a couple of cheroots as he continued. "This atheist gal I know who writes books on religion thinks that Garden of Eden in our Good Book was inspired by some big old oasis long ago in the Holy Land."

Skippy lit up before he joshed, "How could an atheist gal write books about religion, for Pete's sake?"

Longarm shook out the match he'd used to light his own smoke and said, "She claims it makes her objective. Says it's like studying a war when you don't care which side won. I never busted up with her because she never said her prayers. I just found it galling that she was so sure she knew so much about *everything*. I mean, under the simple rules of evidence, the jury is still out on whether we get pie in the sky when we die."

Skippy stared off into space and asked, "Do you reckon poor Hazel went to heaven? She'd led a sort of wild life up until it ended so sudden."

Longarm blew a thoughtful smoke ring and honestly replied, "I don't know. That's why that know-it-all atheist gal galled me. But for what it's worth, she said our human notions of heaven and hell are based on the climates in the old country. She said them Viking folk, stuck up north where they froze their asses in their long dark winters, came up with a hell, the word being Norse, that was cold and dark."

He took another drag and went on. "The Viking notion of heaven was under a roof, warm and cozy, out of the north winds that made their bones creak. But the old-timey folk who wrote *our* Good Book lived in a clime where the worst part of the year was the hot, dry summer, with everybody looking forward to pleasantly cool, wet winters. So the hell they handed down to us is even hotter than the worst weather in desert country, whilst our notions of Eden, or heaven, are more like this well-watered canyon."

"I wish poor Hazel could have made it this far," said Skippy with a sigh.

Longarm nodded and surprised himself a bit as he suddenly found himself murmuring, "The Lord is my shepherd. I shall not want. He maketh me to lie down in green pastures. He leadeth me beside the still waters."

Skippy said, "I'm glad you said that. When Frenchy asks, I mean to tell him we said a prayer before we rode on. *Listening* to a prayer counts as much as saying it, right?"

Longarm shrugged and replied, "I reckon, for all the good either just did for the poor little thing."

Then, since Skippy had been the one who'd brought other members of his gang up, Longarm risked steering

43

the conversation that way, and wound up with a few more mental notes on recent events.

Bragging some, Skippy told Longarm more about that robbery up Colorado way than Longarm had known about from scanning the onionskin transcripts he'd left El Paso with, along with the late Clem Aherne.

The gang had never, as the law assumed, headed for the border to hide out in Old Mexico. They had swell scattered hideouts in Wichita, according to Skippy. They'd assembled there to ride up the Arkansas to rob that bank in Pueblo, Colorado, only to find, once they pulled off their raid smooth as silk and gotten away clean, they were stuck with treasury bonds and other negotiable securities instead of all that ready-cash paper they had been led to expect by the finger, an underpaid and pissed-off Pueblo bank teller.

To cash treasury bonds, railroad or mining stock, and such, you had to take them to another bank when they matured or, to cash them in earlier, take them to a spec-ulator willing to take them off your hands for a fraction of the face value and hold them *until* they matured.

Longarm quietly suggested, "Seems to me you all could have found more than one such jobber there in Kansas."

Skippy said, "Sure we could have. Offering ten cents on the dollar on account the paper was so hot he'd have to hang on to it for years. Sand knew these Mexican money changers willing to offer as high as sixty percent, seeing they couldn't be touched by Uncle Sam when they just took the paper to a regular Mex bank for full re-demption in the sweet by-and-by. Sand said he figured we'd all come out ahead by a grand or more as soon as he could fence the hot paper, see?"

Longarm said, "Not hardly. If you all were so well hid out up Kansas way, how come you all traipsed down to

44

El Paso in a bunch? Why couldn't your slick mastermind pussyfoot down to Old Mexico alone or with, say, a gal tagging along on their honeymoon trip to Old Mexico to cash the hot paper and . . . Never mind. Dumb question, wasn't it?"

Skippy said, "I would have trusted old Sand. He's never done any of us dirty in the past. It was Clem who said we'd all feel safer about our financial future if we all stuck together, see?"

Longarm said he was beginning to as he snuffed out his smoke and laid back on the grass with the big sombrero over his face. Looking up from under the crown at the pinpoints of light in the darkness reminded him of lazy days under another straw hat back in West-by-God Virginia, and it sure was a caution how nostalgic a body could get when he hadn't had much sleep for a spell.

He closed his eyes and let himself drift in the sweet-smelling grass, and that would have been that for a spell had he not suddenly been aware of something bigger than a grasshopper crawling across his tobacco-tweed pants. So he raised the brim of the big sombrero just enough to make sure he knew what he was talking about before he asked, "Skippy, what the fuck is your fucking hand doing on my fucking fly?"

Chapter 6

Skippy snatched his hand away as if Longarm's pants had
suddenly burst into flame. But Longarm sensed he might
have overstated his case when the baby-faced kid with an
old man's eyes said with a pout, "You don't have to get
so huffy about it! Sand told me you done hard time in
Leavenworth and I thought, seeing we were pals and I
was edgy over all this excitement . . ."

Knowing how little he really knew about the outlaw
he was pretending to be, Longarm replied in a more
neighborly tone, "That ain't no way to approach the subject, dammit. If Miss Ellen Terry in the flesh were to grab
at a strange man's cock without warning, she'd be lucky
if she got off with a punch in her pretty mouth."

Skippy sniveled, "Aw, come on, you ain't trying to tell
me you never queered no punks in the big house! Cons
your size don't have to fuck their fist or take it Greek
when it's their turn if they don't want to."

Longarm didn't answer. He left the sombrero in place.
It was easier than trying for a poker face with his upper
lip feeling so curly.

Skippy said, "I don't mind Greek fucking no more.

46

Once you learn to open up and take it like a gal whilst your master plays your trombone for you. I still remember the first time I gave up struggling and all of a sudden it hit me how I was for chrissake getting fucked like a woman, and all of a sudden we were both coming and I was begging for him to do it to me again. Sincere!"

Longarm, as Shadow Manners, muttered, "That was then. It ain't natural after they let you out and you can get at the real thing again. I know a gent ain't supposed to kiss and tell, Skippy, but as a matter of fact I got thoroughly screwed Apache-style last night, and I ain't had a wink of sleep since. So I'll just pass up your kind offer, and for Gawd's sake don't go grabbing without warning anymore!"

Longarm couldn't see his face, but Skippy's voice sure sounded dirty as he said, "I reckon it would be smarter to catch up on some sleep, Shadow. But unless we meet up with some women damn quick, I'm holding you to that offer!"

Longarm didn't answer. He knew it was no use saying he'd made no damned offer to do any damned thing to any damned body.

The big lawman was too sure of his own masculinity to feel any need to brawl with gents of Skippy's persuasion, as long as they were willing to tolerate a man who just couldn't help being queer for women. But having met up with all sorts in his travels, he knew Skippy was one of the pesky ones who couldn't just drop it when he was turned down politely. Following the Owlhoot Trail sure read more romantically in dime novels than in real life. Having jawed with many a convict in his time, Longarm knew all too well how glamorous the adventures of runaway kids could turn out in hobo camps and outlaw hideouts. The new kid in the gang was usually introduced to his new life of crime with a good whupping and a gang

47

rape. If Longarm had his way, *Ned Buntline's Wild West Magazine* would paint more realistic pictures of life along the Owlhoot Trail.

A lot of young gals could use more accurate descriptions of life upon the wicked stage or posing as artists' models for money as well.

In spite of his reservations about a rejected lover packing a gun, Longarm wound up sleeping better than five hours in bits and pieces as the day wore on, and sure enough, they were both hungry as bitch wolves and wide awake by that afternoon.

Longarm suggested, and Skippy agreed, they'd be safer if they went on by daylight where falling off the trail was more likely than having any distant lookout spotting them on it.

Skippy allowed he was glad he'd taken "Shadow's" advice, more than once, as they worked their way down the even-more-treacherous eastern slope. The sun went down just as they reached the gently rolling and craggy stretches of the jumbled-up range. They rode on, and well before midnight they were crossing the wide Tularosa Valley by moonlight.

They knew they didn't have to get all the way across. The SP tracks they were making for ran north and south up the middle. After that things got more complicated.

Unlike the Jornado del Muerto to the west, which looked much the same on a contour map, the Tularosa Valley got more runoff from both the drier San Andres to the west and the way higher and wetter Sacramento and Capitan Mountains. Most of the drainage over yonder ran east into the north-south Pecos Valley, but enough ran west into the Tularosa to inspire many a cattle spread between railroad towns. So as Longarm and Skippy rode across the flats toward Alamogordo, they skirted as close as they dared to the notorious white sands nobody lived on, or rode across, if they had a lick of sense.

They'd long since left the Indian trail Rosario had put them on to. But Skippy was back in familiar territory, he said, so Longarm could only hope he knew what he was doing as they forged on with stirrup-high chaparral to the north and the silvery moonlit dunes of the white sands to their south.

They'd used up the last of their drinking water, sharing most of it with the mules at Longarm's insistence. The Mexican spread where they were to leave the mules lay a short buggy ride west of Alamogordo. The infernal white sands filled a shallow lake bed close to twenty miles across. Along about three A.M. Longarm decided, "These critters are fixing to founder under us if we don't put more water in 'em, pard. I vote we beeline northeast for that dairy farm and bum some water—and with any luck coffee and cake as well!"

Skippy's eyes were good enough to make out the distant lantern light Longarm had indicated. But he showed he had a few things to learn about honest ways of making a living when he asked, "How the hell do you know that's a dairy farm, Shadow?"

Longarm replied, "What else would it be? Who milks beef stock, hogs, or horses at three in the morning? What'll you bet that lamplight's coming from a dairy barn and that they'll be running the fresh milk over to the railroad by four?"

"How do we know they won't turn us in?" asked Skippy.

Longarm snorted. "Why should they? Have you stolen any milk bottles lately? Would you rather explain to the folk in the town ahead why you're coming in off the desert flats afoot after sunrise? Ain't no way in hell we're going to make Alamogordo this side of sunrise, Skippy. But we'll occasion way less gossip if we ride in with a milk wagon as if we know the driver of old."

So Skippy grudgingly agreed, and the two of them headed the three mules toward the distant light. Distances were deceptive in the desert, and so it took them over half an hour to get close enough to matter, and when they had, it was just as well they were too tuckered and thirsty to be chatting. For they'd have been in one hell of a mess if the jaspers they were moving in on had heard them coming.

The first indication anything was wrong came in the form of a woman wailing, *"Por Dios mio, ayúdame!"*

Skippy muttered, "What the fuck?" as they both reined in.

Longarm said, "Grab these reins. Cover me from here!" as he drew the out-of-date but powerful Spencer repeater from his boot.

Skippy was enough of a night rider to shut up and do as he was told while Longarm dismounted silently and moved in on what he now made out as lamplight spilling from the open doorway of a smaller Mexican 'dobe than he'd been picturing.

Two cow ponies with Anglo roping saddles were tethered near the open doorway. Longarm levered a round of .52-40 into the chamber as he eased closer. Before he reached the doorway he could see the limp brown hand of a man down on the dirt floor. If that was his blood all around, he was hit bad. Moving closer, Longarm saw that the middle-aged Mexican spread out on the floor of his humble *casita* had been hit as bad as it got. From the blood spattered on the 'dobe walls and across the dirt floor, they'd done him with that bloody-bladed shovel near his bare feet. The middle-aged woman making all the fuss was getting raped on the bloody dirt floor on the far side of her man. Longarm figured the grinning dog watching with a Henry repeater in his hands was the most dangerous of the pair to himself. So he shot him first as he stepped into the light.

Thanks to the big 410-grain round being backed by no more powder than a Winchester .44's two hundred grains, the effect was paradoxical. The big slug stayed in the son of a bitch to lift him off his feet and bounce him off the far wall, killed by the hydrostatic shock before he landed facedown across his Henry.

The one left scrambled off the woman he'd been abusing like a scalded cat, yelling, "I give! I give! For the love of God I give!" as he fumbled his pants up.

Addressing the owl-eyed woman on the floor in Spanish, Longarm told her he was her servant. She spat out, *"Matalo!"* So the Spencer went off again, and the rapist wound up propped against that same far wall with his dead legs draped over the rump of his pal.

The woman was naturally crying fit to bust, with her dead husband's head in her lap and one tit still hanging out of her torn cotton shift, when Skippy joined them with his own Yellowboy loaded and locked. The baby-faced kid with the eyes of an old man marveled, "What the fuck?"

Longarm said, "That's about the size of it. Them two saddle tramps wanted the modest opportunities offered by this chicken ranch or whatever. The light we spotted was their notion of added enjoyment, not a herd of cows being milked."

Skippy said, "Aw, shit, they were just poor greasers and she ain't even good-looking!"

Longarm replied, "That's what I just said. Watch your mouth. This poor woman has suffered insults enough for one night. What have you done with the mules?"

Skippy said, "Tethered them beside them two ponies, of course. But we'd best be on our way, Shadow. We

51

ain't more than a few miles out of town and rifle shots do echo across the flats at night!"

Longarm said, "It's no wonder you've spent enough hard time so you like it Greek! Use your head! The town law is on its way even as we speak. We don't want to meet up with them without this witness to our innocence. Fetch her some water and find a washrag to wet for her whilst I see what I can do to comfort her."

Between them, they couldn't do half what the poor old gal wanted. But Longarm convinced her to tidy up with the damp rag, and got her into a fresh cotton shift, although she refused to sit anywhere but on her knees with her man's bloody head in her lap. So Longarm started putting their humble overturned furniture in place. Working in close quarters with that big straw sombrero on was awkward, so he placed it on the sky-blue table he'd set back on its legs. The two of them had just dragged the dead rapists out into the dooryard by their heels when they heard a distant shot, and a gruff voice rang out, "Undersheriff J. Weddington Barrow of Otero County here, and somebody better have an explanation for them recent gunshots at four in the fucking morning!"

Longarm murmured, "Let me do the talking, Mr. Wilson," before he called back, "That was my gun you heard! Name's Crawford. My sidekick here is Skip Wilson. We just now busted up a gang rape. Got here too late to prevent a murder. Lady in the house can tell you more than we can, seeing she's one of the victims and knows where we are right now!"

The undersheriff and his six hastily gathered followers rode closer, with Barrow warning, "Keep them hands polite whilst we see what Señora Galvez has to say for you. Them two at your feet the ones you just now accused?"

Longarm allowed that was about the size of it as

Skippy whispered, "Who the fuck is Skip Wilson? When did you turn into a Crawford? Neither name means shit to me and I know most everybody in the business!"

Longarm muttered, "That's the general idea, you asshole. We ain't in the business. We're honest young punchers looking for work. Got laid off down West Texas way. Heard they might be hiring up around Fort Stanton. So shut up and stay shut, dammit!"

Skippy didn't dare another word as the burly undersherrif and his boys reined in and dismounted to admire the dead rapists spread out in the dooryard dust. Before Longarm could explain further, Barrow called to one of his own, "Fernando, go inside and get a statement from Señora Galvez, without any helpful hints from these gents we've never seen before."

As a slender Mexican-American headed for the lamplit doorway, Barrow had a second thought and said, "Injun Pete, go with him and scout for signs that may or may not go with anybody's statements."

The two deputies ducked inside. From the wails that came out the door, the mistreated lady of the house knew Fernandez well enough to yell in Spanish that one of the beasts who killed her Pablo had been trying to shove it up her *culo*.

Longarm spoon-fed the lawmen outside his hastily made-up story. The older undersheriff only commenced to thaw when his Indian tracker came out of the house holding that big straw sombrero.

Barrow whistled and said, "Sweet Jesus in the manger! We got an all-points wire about a jasper wearing a hat like so gunning a federal prisoner aboard the D&RG and likely dry-gulching a famous federal lawman in the desert earlier this very week! Which one of them was wearing that famous sombrero, Crawford?"

Longarm truthfully replied, "Hats went flying all over

53

when I tore in to bust things up rapid-fire. Does it matter now, seeing they're both . . . retired?"

Barrow chortled. "I see it all now. Whichever one wore that hat aboard the train shot the man they'd sent him after, pulled the cord, and jumped in the Jornado del Muerto to find his partner waiting with them two cow ponies. Them cow ponies were the mounts they were riding, right?"

Longarm said, "I reckon. Me and my sidekick rode north with these good old saddle mules. Knowing they'd see us across dry range safer and with an eye to selling them or swapping them for ponies farther north."

Barrow was hardly listening as he mused half to himself, "*Bueno.* These two killers pushed over the San Andres on horseback, abusing said horses in the process. So they stopped here to see if Galvez had any fresher stock, remembered they hadn't been getting any lately, and proceeded to rape the poor old greaser's wife!"

He grinned at Longarm and added, "It's a good thing you boys came along just in time, Crawford."

Before Longarm could modestly reply, Injun Pete, standing there pensively with that big sombrero, chimed in. "Hear me. I have a question. These two riders who saved Señora Galvez say they rode up here from West Texas with those three mules. Why would two men ride three mules, and why is one of the mules carrying a side-saddle?"

Chapter 7

Longarm replied with ease he didn't feel, "Them vaquero saddles came with the stock as part of the same deal. Do we look like dally-roping Mexican hands? We bought the kit and caboodle off a hard-up Mexican called Robles, I think, who need *dinero* sudden to take home to his *mujer* after an unlucky run of cards. We never asked why one of 'em was sidesaddled. Might have been his *mujer*'s mount. Figured we'd carry it along to sell along with the two vaqueros. Must have cost somebody forty dollars new."

Fernando, the deputy who'd just spoken to the upset woman inside, let fly with a disgusted snort and said, "*Pendejo,* these Anglos are the ones who avenged the death of Galvez to save the honor of his widow. What do you care for how they came by *mierda*? Has anybody reported the theft of that stock or those saddles?"

Injun Pete said, "I just find it odd when two riders say they rode from West Texas with a woman's empty saddle on a third mule."

Longarm said, "Have it your way. I cannot tell a lie. A pretty little thing run off with us, but we lost her along the way when she fell into a hole in the ground."

Undersheriff Barrow chimed in. "Cut the bullshit and let's tidy up out here." He ordered two of his men to ride into town and fetch the coroner. Turning back to Longarm and Skippy, he said, "You two can ride on in for now. But don't plan on riding on before the coroner allows you can. Where will you be staying in Alamogordo in case we need you before the inquest?"

Skippy wailed, "We can't stay in Alamogordo that long! We got to get on up to . . ."

"We just got here. We'll have to let you know where to find us once we find someplace to stay," Longarm cut in, stepping on Skippy's foot before he could put it in his mouth.

Barrow curtly replied, "See you do that then. I ain't expecting nobody to be charged with shooting skunks out of season. But they'll want your signed depositions before you ride on."

Longarm said he had to get his hat, and ducked inside just long enough to choose the newest Stetson on the dirt floor. The weeping woman with a dead man's head in her lap never looked up. So he just quit while he was ahead.

Outside, he suggested she could use a doctor. Barrow said the deputy coroner who'd be coming on out was a real M.D. So Longarm got himself and Skippy out of there before anybody could ask any more awkward questions.

As they rode out of earshot, Skippy said, "I admire a man who can think on his feet. You surely bullshit fine, Shadow. Once we make her to town and tell our pals we made it, all of us will light out by rail for Kansas!"

Longarm sighed and said, "You must really like being in jail. Didn't they ever tell you the first rule of riding the Owlhoot Trail was not to draw attention to your being *on* it?"

Skippy replied, "Sure. I just said we go along with your bullshit till we can catch us a train on out. Who's going to pay attention to us after we're long gone?"

Longarm said, "Otero County, once it notices it has two dead bodies and a fishy story to cope with. Out-of-work-but-innocent drifting hands would have no call to run off after the law distinctly ordered them to stay put. For all they'd know, there could have been bounty money posted on two *buscaderos* they'd just gunned legal."

Skippy said, "I never gunned shit. You'd dropped 'em both before I got in the door."

Longarm said, "Whatever. The point is, it would look suspicious as all hell if we lit out before a pro forma hearing, and Mr. Morse invented a telegraph to send word up and down any railroad line about suspicious passengers Otero County would like another word with. So first we unload these suspicious mules where Rosario asked us to. Then we wake your pals up to tell 'em we made it, and if Sand and the others want to go on, once he pays me the rest of my fee for Clem Aherne, I'll be proud to sit tight in Alamogordo, take a bow at the coroner's inquest for doing the right thing, and be on my own way."

Skippy eagerly suggested, "I never saw nothing back yonder. Can't you tell them that for me if I go home to Kansas with the bunch?"

Longarm shrugged and allowed nobody was likely to press the matter as long as the one owning up to the gun-play showed up. So they rode on, with Longarm's mind in a whirl.

For despite his easy manner, they were coming to the endgame fast. His shithouse run of luck had to run out the moment the man who'd hired Shadow Manners to gun his captured sidekick laid eyes on what Skippy had brought back instead.

But what the hell, thought Longarm, he'd have the

57

edge of knowing a storm was on the way before any of them heard the first roll of thunder. The idea was to gather as many nuggets of information as he could before he had to break cover and arrest the survivors.

So when they made it on in by the tricky light of cock's crow, they went first to the goat farm fronting for a horse thief called Moreno on the outskirts of town. The place was easy to find because as Rosario had told them, Moreno had two sun-bleached goat skulls above his gate, one on each post, with a whitewashed wagon wheel leaning against the barbed wire on the inside, as if kids had been playing with it.

Moreno, a beefy mestizo, who obviously ate well for a goat farmer, was naturally up and about at that hour. Tourists who dismissed the dozing Mexican one saw in the sunlight as lazy didn't savvy the hours folks stuck in hot sunny climates followed.

When he learned about the killings out at the Galvez place, Moreno was of a mind that their transaction was over. He said he'd see Rosario got his stock back and suggested they get off his propery pronto.

But as the two of them walked into town, which was distinguished by the awesome tree stumps that had once given the water stop a name meaning fat or thick cotton-woods, Longarm had another name and address filed away for the law. He meant to play Skippy like a fish on the line until he could find out where outlaws hid out right in town before he commenced a final fandango. Waiting for Sand Lachlan, an outlaw he didn't know on sight, to notice they'd never met before was too big a boo. But it was a shame he wouldn't be able to follow the chain of way stations all the way north to what seemed to be a network of safe addresses for outlaws in Kansas. Putting Sand Lachlan and his inner circle away would have to do. Once they rounded up Carillo, Rosario, and Moreno, a lot

58

of seedy shelter operators were sure to get away. But what the hell, you ate the apple one bite at a time.

Since Skippy had hung on to the Yellowboy after surrendering the saddle borrowed from the local crooks, Longarm had found it easy to stroll on with the seven-shot Spencer as well as his .44-40 and double derringer. He was figuring the awesome muzzle of the powerful Spencer would freeze everybody if he just swung it up to cover them as he declared they were all under arrest. After questioning Skippy casually, he figured there'd be Sand Lachlan himself, along with no more than four other men and most likely as many women. Ten to one odds, counting Skippy and the doxies, didn't sound so bad when you started out with the drop on the bunch.

Skippy led him past the railroad stop at dawn, and opened the gate of a picket-fenced dooryard. Inside was what Skippy described as a boardinghouse, combining Mexican 'dobe walls with the white trim and two-story vernanda of the Old South. Skippy had said the place belonged to somebody called Texas Red.

As they mounted the steps, Longarm kept the Spencer's muzzle down at a polite angle. It wasn't easy. Despite his outward calm, his heart inside was hammering hard enough to shingle the barn and his tongue felt dry and tasty as an old sock. Skippy opened the unlocked front door to lead Longarm in as if they owned the place. Longarm found himself in a two-story-tall foyer, facing a bodacious spiral staircase. A tall figure in green velvet was coming down the stairs under a pinned-up mop of what looked like fresh-peeled carrots. As the three of them met at the foot of the stairs, she said, "It's about time you got here, Skippy! Is this moose you brought along Shadow Manners?"

Skippy snorted, "Who else might I be leading in on

you, Texas Red? Does he look like a lawman I met up with along the way?"

Texas Red smiled thinly at Longarm and replied, "As a matter of fact he could pass for one, you shifty-eyed squirt." Then she held out a hand and added, "Put her there, Shadow! I've heard bad things about you and that's all right with me, because there ain't nobody badder than *this* child!"

Longarm had to shift the Spencer to his left hand to shake. As he did so he admired Texas Red. If you liked your eggs and women hard-boiled, she was a handsome specimen, too firm of jaw and heavy of brow to call pretty. But she surely filled that green velvet nicely, and it seemed a shame she'd be spending the night in jail.

Skippy asked where everybody else might be. Texas Red said, "Left last night on the northbound sleeper. Sand heard there were two tough-looking strangers in town. Once he made sure they weren't talking about the two of you, he considered bounty hunters, balanced that against the time he'd allowed you boys and Hazel, and . . . By the way, where's Hazel?"

Skippy said, "Dead. It was a natural accident. Nobody knows but us. I suspect Shadow here might have shot those two mysterious strangers, though!"

Texas Red suggested they continue the conversation around some breakfast and led them back to her big boardinghouse dining room as Skippy went on filling her in on the shoot-out at the Galvez spread.

The tall redhead rang a table bell, and preened, sort of pleased, when Longarm held her chair for her. The three of them had barely settled at the table before a pretty young Mexican gal appeared out of nowhere with a coffee urn in one hand as she balanced a tray of cups, saucers, and many a doughnut with the other. As she poured Longarm's cup, he could smell the brandy. It smelled better to him than the chickory folks mixed in their so-called French coffee down along the Gulf where houses came with two-story verandas. Texas Red talked more Bluegrass than Old Plantation. The doughnuts were just plain doughnuts, a New England invention currently as widespread as Mom's apple pie from Frankonia by way of Pennsylvania, although now served with English "American" cheese.

As they ate, Texas Red agreed that Undersheriff Barrow would likely raise Ned by telegraph if the shooters he'd trusted skipped out on him. Skippy brought up his notion that "Shadow" was the only one they'd really care about. When Texas Red said it wouldn't kill him to stay upstairs with Shadow till after the fool hearing, Longarm demurred. "They ain't likely to make a fuss if Skippy goes on, Miss Red. Like Skippy says and as I can assure them, he was outside, holding our mounts, when I walked in on those rascals. The Widow Galvez will back us on that if push comes to shove. After that, the fewer of us the law can question the less chance we'll have to trip one another up. Riding alone, I'll be free to whip up any fool answers to questions I might not be expecting."

The statuesque redhead shrugged her square shoulders and decided it was none of her beeswax how they wanted to settle it.

Skippy chortled, "Hot damn! Ain't there a northbound due through here this side of high noon, Texas Red?"

When she nodded, Longarm said, "Not so fast, Skippy. You boys still owe this child two hundred and fifty for a job well done. You can tell Sand that missing lawman's on me, but he owes me on Aherne."

Then, since it was easy to hold the reins so gently, Longarm turned to their hostess to ask, "Old Sand didn't leave my money with you, did he, ma'am?"

Texas Red said, "Perish the thought! I provide room

61

and board for boys like you. I neither take part nor want to know that much about your need for discreet transient shelter!"

Longarm nodded as if thinking, turned to Skippy, and said, "You'd best give me some address I can drop by, once I get on up to Wichita myself."

Skippy answered easily, "You'll find me easy enough. I room above the Franco-Turkish Baths near the station."

"How about Sand?" Longarm asked.

Skippy replied, "How's about me knowing by the time you look me up in Wichita where Sand wants to meet up with you in Wichita? You know what a temper he has, and how uncertain it can explode."

Longarm let it go, now that he had yet another address to file away. As he washed down another doughnut with inspiring coffee, he reflected on how the enforced delay there in Alamogordo might be shaped to his own advantage.

To begin with, he'd have plenty of opportunities to wire coded messages to his home office in Denver. Scouting up Sand Lachlan with some backup had to have barging in alone beat.

So the three of them were in a relaxed mood by the time that northbound train and *la siesta* got close enough to study on. The brandy in their coffee helped.

Consulting his pocket watch, Longarm told Skippy, "I've skipped some towns in my time, so listen tight. Leave me and your Yellowboy here and sort of drift over to the station as if you might be meeting somebody or just like to look at trains. If you spot anybody staked out by the tracks, come on back after you let one train pass your innocent self by. If nobody seems to be watching, wait till the All Aboard, count to Mississippi sixty times, and board as the train starts up. When the conductor asks, tell him you didn't get a chance to buy your ticket in town and bet him he can't sell you one aboard the train. He'll assure you he can and the Southern Pacific may or may not see any money you give him."

He let that sink in before he added, "Find a seat, sit down, and don't talk to nobody this side of Carrizozo."

"What's in Carrizozo?" Skippy asked.

Longarm said, "Lincoln County. If nobody there takes you off the train for *this* county, you can figure you're free and clear. You'd better start drifting. You don't want to look like you're anxious to get anywheres."

Skippy rose, they shook on that, and the baby-faced kid with an old man's eyes left for Kansas, walking a tad unsteadily.

After he'd gone, Texas Red started to pour more brandy-laced coffee, decided she'd had enough for now, and asked, "Won't you be in a pickle if that little pansy gets picked up and they question him where you can't hear?"

Longarm didn't consider it was the time to tell her he could always get out his badge and identification in such an emergency. Stalling for time, he just shrugged and said, "I 'spect he'll make it, and to tell the truth he was making me edgy. I'll feel better dancing with the coroner with Skippy off the floor."

Texas Red smiled dirty and asked, "Did he offer to blow your French horn for you, Shadow? I've heard he likes to."

Longarm shrugged and replied, "I never discuss my music lessons with anyone after class."

To which Texas Red replied in a sort of purr, "I'm so glad to know you feel that way, Shadow. A girl such as I has to consider her reputation and some riders gossip so dirty along the Owlhoot Trail!"

Chapter 8

"How in the hell did we wind up in this swell position?" asked Texas Red as they shared a cheroot propped up in her four-poster, naked as a couple of jaybirds and closer to sober.

Longarm didn't answer as he blew a little smoke ring through a bigger one. It wouldn't have been polite to ask if she'd bought in to the bullshit about nobody being allowed to testify in court against anybody who'd ever gone down on them, or whether, in truth, she'd been telling the truth in her cups downstairs about never going upstairs with an outlaw guest when she had others under the same roof.

From the way she'd just been acting, Longarm thought it safe to assume her place had been sheltering lots of owlhoot riders for a spell. He'd long since learned folks in the habit of answering questions with care were inclined to tell you more when you didn't press them to tell you more than they felt like spilling.

He told her how swell she screwed as he snuggled her closer and pressed the cheroot to her lips. So as if she felt he was trying to shut her up, she took a quick drag and passed the smoke back, asking, "How long do you think we have together before they hold that hearing, darling?"

He truthfully answered, "Can't say for certain. If they don't hold her this side of Friday morn, we've likely a whole weekend like this, if I'm man enough."

She slickered her long smooth curves against him as she purred, "Oh, you're man enough and you know it, Shadow! I could tell the first thrust you treated me to that this would be the beginning of a beautiful friendship. How did you satisfy all you have to offer a girl whilst you were in Leavenworth that time?"

He said, "It wasn't easy."

She said, "I'm not one to pass judgment. I spent close to five years in a girls' reform school, just as I'd learned about fucking, so I guess I know how it feels to . . . satisfy yourself and a cell mate as best you can. But tell me something, Shadow. It's not that I mind at all, but I noticed as we were . . . getting to know one another, you're hung bigger than average. So didn't the boys you buggered in Leavenworth find it a tad rough on the smaller invitations they had to extend?"

He shrugged and said, "One such inviting cuss I talked to a spell back said he got a boot out of feeling used and abused, the way some gals like a brutal lover."

Texas Red reached down to fondle his semi-satisfied manhood as she purred, "I don't like a man to rough me up. I tend to hit back. But what you just had in me, moving with consideration, felt so grand I Jesus H. Christ want *more*! Let me get on top and see if we can get it in soft and bring it to full attention again!"

They found they could. Although Longarm wound up on top before they were done that time. As he paused for breath, letting it soak where she wanted it, Texas Red sobbed. "Oh, no, you can't go on to Kansas as soon as next week! I ain't expecting any more customers to hide for a couple of weeks. Say you'll bide with me like this at least that long!"

Longarm kissed the part in her unbound red hair and gently told her that nobody riding the Owlhoot Trail made plans that far ahead. Then he sniffed and added, "Hold on, I smell a sheep on fire!"

He disengaged from her clinging limbs to roll over to the edge of the bed and find that that cheroot they'd lost track of was burning a hole in the wool rug.

He swore, swung his bare feet to the rug, and reached for the water pitcher on the bed-side table as he said, "This'll learn us not to smoke when fucking!"

Texas Red peered over the edge beside him on her hands and knees, then laughed and said, "It's out. You want to put it in again doggy-style?"

So that felt swell too, and the contrast between her lean white body by daylight, patterned in floral patterns of light and shadow through her lace curtains, and the tawny candlelit charms of the Mescalero stoop-tag artist, inspired some thrusting Texas Red found mighty flattering.

So a good time was had by all until, as all things good and bad must, it ended for the moment in a mutual climax he felt down to the soles of his feet while she yowled like an alley cat in heat.

So they slept that one off, with her shapely naked body spooned in his flushed flesh as they lay on their sides, until all of a sudden he got to wondering how he could be trying to sneak it up into good old Roping Sally at that angle, Roping Sally being murdered and all.

As full realization stood his hair on end, he opened his eyes to find with considerable relief that he didn't have it half inside a buxom blond corpse after all. Then the mighty warm and active redhead arched her spine to take it deeper, even as she sighed and said, "I'm too hungry for something to eat and I am talking about eating *food*. What time is it, darling?"

Longarm glanced at the window curtains and decided, "You're right. Must be going on supper time, and setting fire to your rug ain't the only mess I might have made here in Alamogordo. I clean forgot I gave my word I'd let the local law know where to find me."

"You mean to tell the law about me and my business?" she gasped as she slid off his dick entirely.

He explained, "They don't have me and Skippy down as gents on the dodge. They bought us being out-of-work hands drifting north to look for work up Fort Stanton way. If you'd rather, I could find some other place here in town. But I don't see how—"

"I don't see how either, and you're not getting away from this girl that easy!" she cut in. "I am listed as a boardinghouse keeper on the county tax rolls. Let's talk about it whilst I start supper down to the kitchen."

He said he had a better idea. She agreed he'd have a better excuse to cut his visit to the sheriff's substation short if he had his supper waiting in her respectable boardinghouse.

So they got up and got dressed, and things came up roses for Longarm that evening in Alamogordo.

None of the lawmen he'd talked to out at the Galvez spread were on duty that close to supper time. The night watch commander he jawed with had heard about the killings, of course, and been instructed to take down any address "Mr. Crawford" or "Mr. Wilson" might offer. He said the widow Chavez had kin out to her farm to help her with things. The late Pablo Chavez was to be planted over by the old Mexican mission come Sunday.

The night man never blinked an eye when Longarm told him in a desperately casual tone, "My sidekick, Wilson, went on ahead to Fort Stanton lest we lose the jobs we were on our way to apply for. Like I told Undersheriff Barrow, I was the one who gunned those rapists and Wilson never saw much. I can wire him to come on back, if the coroner needs him bad enough to pay our expenses home if he fails to nail them jobs down for us."

The night man said, "I'll pass that on. Don't see them needing Wilson's testimony for an open-and-shut case of justifiable. You say you'll be at the Widow Fulton's boardinghouse near the station?"

Longarm said that was about the size of it. He still didn't know the true first name of Texas Red. The local lawman asked, "Notice anything odd about any of her other boarders, Mr. Crawford?"

Longarm truthfully replied, "Ain't seen any. Got the feeling business was slow and she was glad to see us. I hope you ain't implying I'm staying in a house of ill repute!"

The night watch comander easily replied, "Don't know what she might be running. Folk here in town have reported all sorts of odd birds going in and out at odd hours. Barrow says he don't know what to make of that big redhead. She ain't from around here. Texas gal, I hear tell."

Longarm broke out a couple of smokes as he chuckled and observed, "I noticed she was redheaded and good-looking. Coming from *Texas* likely adds up to something worse. Far be it from me to question neighborhood gossip, but for what it's worth, ain't nobody boarding with her but me right now, so I'll try not to act too odd."

The local lawman laughed, Longarm lit his smoke for him first, and they parted friendly.

It was going on sundown, when the light got tricky as it ever could, when Longarm made sure nobody was tailing him and crossed over to enter the Alamogordo Western Union.

Longarm and his boss, Marshal Billy Vail, had long since worked out a simple double code for night-letter wires they'd as soon keep private. It involved the sort of inside sarcasm parents used when they didn't want the kids to know the details of Big Sister's pending shotgun wedding.

Tearing off a long night-letter form, Longarm began by block-lettering, "SORRY TO TAKE SO LONG TO LET YOU KNOW NEPHEW IS ALIVE AND WELL AFTER PARTY BUSTED UP BY RUDE FURRINER CALLED RGZCNY LZMMDQR IF I SPELLED IT RIGHT STOP . . ." with names encoded by using the letter before the actual letter, save for the first letter, A, which was naturally Z. The real Z being Y. He kept his message as terse as possible, but made sure Billy got all the names and map coordinates he'd noted so far, sending those compass points as they'd read on the map.

A cryptographer with military training could no doubt break their code if he suspected it *was* a code. But few telegraphers inclined to gossip in saloon were likely to give a shit about the comings and goings of a mooncalf who seemed to hang out with "furriners."

Getting back to the boardinghouse in the gloaming, Longarm was met in the doorway with a French kiss and an invite to supper. As they were served at the big empty table by the kitchen help, Longarm hedged his bets by telling her right out he'd been to the Western Union to see if Skippy had wired he was in trouble.

Texas Red allowed she'd expected the pansy to make it, and let slip one more gang secret when she added, "I understand he lives in sin with a towel boy in some Wichita bathhouse. Sand Lachlan won't stand for flagrant fruit-picking around that high-toned Dexter Hotel he stays at."

Longarm managed not to jump up and lay her on the table. He wasn't supposed to show so much delighted surprise at things gang members would be expected to know. But she'd just handed him the gang on a silver platter! He wouldn't have to con his way within shooting range of a ruthless gang leader after all. Knowing where the bastard roomed in Wichita, he only had to give them time to settle down before he led a posse of federal and Kansas lawmen to round them up in the wee small hours!

It was as good as over. He wouldn't have to go through the charade of appearing before that local coroner's jury under a made-up name. He was free to just produce his badge, tell Undersheriff Barrow what was really going on, and make a deal. Barrow would no doubt be proud to tend to the paperwork for the killing out at the Galvez spread in exchange for this one way station on the Owlhoot Trail, and Longarm could get on up to Wichita and fix the clock of the son of a bitch who'd killed a federal prisoner he'd been expected to deliver alive in Denver.

"Could you use more gravy on your mashed potatoes, darling?" Texas Red was asking, breaking into his thoughts just as they were getting around to her.

He said his spuds were fine, and cut more steak as he pictured how she was going to look at him when it came time to teach her screwing a lawman didn't offer immunity from the law.

He knew he was going to feel like a shit. He knew from her point of view he'd *be* a shit. But she'd chosen of her own free will to be a crook. Or to aid and abet crooks, which was just as serious in the eyes of the law. Longarm knew his biggest problem enforcing the law was his sense of *equity*, a notion that had never applied in the Roman law that common law was based on.

That was how come the Roman lawmen who'd arrested that general for high treason had had to rape his seven-year-old daughter whether they'd felt like it or not. Under Roman law a traitor's whole family had to be nailed up to crosses to either side of him. So that included seven-year-olds, but then, since under the same Roman law nobody could execute a *virgin,* they had to make sure the terrified child lost her virginity before they nailed her up to die beside her father.

Longarm only knew that because insisting the law was the law, with no ifs, ands, or buts, could lead to results so sickening that Roman lawyers themselves wrote down what had happened.

A Roman judge who'd passed the sentence had stained his court records with his own tears as he'd written about a child being crucified while promising to be good if only they'd tell her what she'd done wrong.

So over the years since, the principle of equity, or "Let's be sensible," had crept into common law, beginning with not holding the family of any felon liable for the crime.

Self-defense and other forms of justifiable killing came under the sort of hazy rules of equity. Courts could reduce the usual punishments by considering mitigating circumstances such as being *loco en la cabeza* or having kids at home on the verge of starvation. But as Billy Vail had warned his senior deputy more than once, such excuses were for the courts to decide, not the arresting officer.

So when Texas Red asked, "What's wrong, honey bun? You look like poor Inez put too much salt in your food!" Longarm could only answer, "The grub's just fine. I've been mulling over something they let slip when I was over to the substation earlier."

She asked what it was, of course.

He said, "They may be on to you. Made mention of gossip here in town about you mayhaps hiding crooks out here. They don't know *I'm* a crook, and I was able to tell 'em you weren't hiding nobody over here but me."

Texas Red tried to put a brave face on it as she laughed

71

and warned him how she meant to keep him boarding with her all summer.

He said he meant to make her regret that promise once he got her up the stairs. But then he said, "Serious-like, pretty lady, you got to know when to hold and when to fold, and once the law gets to sniffing round a tree, it's time to quit pissing on it. If I was running this stopover on the Owlhoot Trail and I even *guessed* they were getting on to me, I reckon I'd sell the place for what I could get and get the blue blazes out of the state!"

She blanched and asked, "Do you really think it's that serious, Shadow?"

He said, "If I'm wrong, what have you lost by moving on? If they're on to you, it could cost you more time licking pussy with your cell mate!"

She gulped and decided, "One thing's for certain. I meant to wire a certain party his reservations here have just been canceled."

She sipped more coffee laced with brandy before she added with a nod of resignation, "I could likely get as much as I paid for this place, now that I've cleaned it out and tidied it up."

So Longarm was able to look Texas Red in the eye the next time they went at it face-to-face with the bedroom lamp still lit, and didn't just putting a place like hers out of business count for something, next to feeling like a shit-eating dog when you didn't really have to?

Chapter 9

Fornication with a friendly redhead felt even better when a man had a clear conscience about the way he was screwing her. Thursday morning Texas Red had a For Sale sign posted out front. By the time he got back from jawing with Undersheriff Barrow some more, she said she'd had a couple of nibbles. She'd bought a sort of seedy *posada* handy to the railroad, and spruced it up to where anyone with a lick of business sense could see it was a valuable property now.

It wasn't easy. But Longarm managed not to pontificate on the wages of sin. He wasn't supposed to be a lawman who'd seen how one poor soul after another had wasted life and freedom chasing what looked like easy money right past the end of the rainbow.

Counting unprofitable misery from time spent in prison, the average rider of the Owlhoot Trail made no more money in his often shorter lifetime than any day laborer willing to work that hard as soon as you deducted expenses of a life on the dodge no day laborer had to pay.

A cowhand drawing a dollar a day got to pocket the whole dollar, sleeping most nights in a bunkhouse at no expense after a supper provided by the outfit. Folks such as Texas Red who fed and sheltered holdup men on the dodge charged more than the best hotels and restaurants for what was often rotten cooking and literally lousy bedding. Texas Red was more expensive than most, as well as far fancier than average.

"Shadow Manners" confessed, and she was pleased to hear, that he'd have had a time meeting her prices if she hadn't stopped charging him. She seemed to feel screwing her boarders would make her a whore. He was glad she felt like that. The thought of going sloppy seconds to the murderous Sand Lachlan hadn't appealed to him at all.

Thursday night was swell. When they told him Friday afternoon that the hearing would be held come Monday, he reflected on how Texas Red kept letting things slip about Sand Lachlan's gang and other gangs as well. So he assured himself Billy Vail would expect him to ride his run of luck out. Figuring a man would have to just do his duty over the weekend, Longarm never told them who he was. He'd decided on following through as far as he could, and a shy Mexican kid had come by to hand El Señor Crawford a handpress-printed invitation, in Spanish, to the funeral of the late Pablo Galvez. Texas Red had said she'd have to think about going along. She got along all right with her hired gals, but her mama's folks had lost kin in that Mexican War.

Longarm dropped by the Western Union to see if there were messages from Skippy Steiner or his uncle Bill from Denver. There'd come nothing from Skippy, meaning he hadn't been picked up, and Uncle Billy advised his nephew to keep up the good work and wire the address in Alamogordo where that "furrin" gal, the Widow Etksnm, lived because they had a swell bracelet for her birthday.

Longarm wired back that it wasn't that "furrin" gal's birthday just yet, and headed back to the boardinghouse to see how Texas Red was doing with her For Sale sign.

He didn't see it when he turned in at her gate. One of her serving gals, the pretty one called Catalina, was sitting on the front steps in her white cotton shift, looking like an abandoned waif. As Longarm approached, she jumped to her sandal-shod feet to hold out an envelope Texas Red had left him. "La Tejana Roja is no more here! She tell me for to give you this!"

Longarm took the letter with a nod of thanks, and tore it open to read as he propped one boot on the steps:

My Darling:

Forgive me for not parting with sweeter sorrow but I have learned the hard way to strike while the iron was hot! I got a more generous offer for the property, furnishings and all, than expected. So I've come out ahead and I'm heading out for the hills before the waters rise any higher. I've had Inez run me up to the next flag stop lest anyone here be watching at the station. It's been grand. I'll never forget you. What else can I say?

Your wicked playmate

P.S. The new owners won't take possession until Monday, so think of me in our love nest tonight if you like. My help will be staying on with the new owners. I told them to serve you until you leave.

Folding the note and tucking it away, Longarm asked Catalina why she was crying, adding, "Says here you and Inez still have a job and a roof over your head. You know the folks who've bought the place?"

She nodded and said, "They are Anglos, *pero simpatico*. I do not weep for worry about me *empleo*. I weep for because I thought she loved me, and first she sleep

75

with you instead of me, and now she go away without she even kiss me!"

Longarm shot a thoughtful look down at her, managed not to grin as he pictured a tawny little gal in her teens tangled bare-ass with a long, lean pale-skinned redhead, and muttered, "Well, she said she'd spent hard time and had to be more discreet with most male guests. So what's for supper, seeing you seem to be in charge of the place for tonight, Miss Catalina?"

She said with a pout that Inez did most of the cooking, and wasn't expected back until after midnight because *La Patrona* was out to flag down that night train north. But when Longarm said he'd try the chili joint over by that Western Union, she said, "*Pero no!* Anyone can make chili better than that fat chihuahua who calls herself a *cocinera Mejicana*! I will not have you poisoned just for sleeping with La Tejana Roja. *La cena* will be served in one hour!"

So they went inside and parted friendly in the foyer. Longarm went up to the room he'd been sharing with Texas Red, and carried the two rifles down to leave by the front door, more to kill time than from any sense of urgency. He figured on unloading both at a hockshop he'd noticed up the way for some extra pocket jingle. A man on the road could never have more pocket jingle than he needed as one damn surprise came up after another.

Not feeling like the Prince of Wales waiting to be served in his fat old palace, Longarm moseyed out to the kitchen to see if he could give Catalina a hand. She said with a pout that she didn't need any help with the chili con carne she was whipping up. But when he tasted it, she did.

Taking off his hat and coat to hang on a pantry hook, Longarm rolled up his sleeves as he told her, "You've gotten too used to cooking for Anglo riders raised on grits and gravy. Cooks along the border, whether Mex or Tex, seem to have a contest on and use more pepper than Professor Darwin ever resolved the human stomach to cope with. But the chili cools sensible as you move either north or south from the border, and I like my ground beef and beans seasoned about the latitude of the Arkansas River."

He grabbed a fistful of dried red peppers to crunch up like autumn leaves, and dropped them into the milder potion she had steaming on the cast-iron range as he added, "You can stir if you like. You got any white sugar around here? I know it sounds wrong, but a few spoons of sugar seems to spread the heat more evenly in any hot sauce."

She told him to stir while she fetched sugar from the pantry. So he did. When she rejoined him, she asked with renewed interest just how much sugar he wanted to stir in.

After he'd explained you were using too much if you could taste it, Catalina smiled up at him for the first time and observed that he seemed to know all sorts of ways to sweeten things sneaky.

When he just went on stirring, she confided, "Inez and me listened at the door and tried not for to laugh out loud. What did La Tejana Roja mean when she say was time for to give the poor dog a bone?"

Longarm stirred on with a shrug and replied, "Ain't certain. You know how childish we all talk at such times. I reckon half the fun is getting to forget whe're supposed to act like grown-ups. You say . . . you and that older cook share such secrets, Miss Catalina?"

The sultry little mestiza smiled like Miss Mona Lisa after hearing a lie and confessed, "La Tejana Roja say she love Inez too. Was Inez she hired first. I was invited for to join their *hermanadad secreta* after I walked in on them one morning. They both said they loved me. Inez was most times the *muchacho, pero* sometimes was my turn."

She looked away with a sigh and continued. "I do not know if I was good at that or not. Inez and that bent *candelero* inside both of us was close as I have ever done it with real *muchachos*."

Longarm couldn't help laughing as he pictured her deflowering by the older and fatter Inez.

Catalina flared. "Is not my fault I am not a woman of more experience! *La Patrona* said she would fire us if she ever caught us in bed with any of her guests. Inez risked it a few times, Inez is crazy between her legs. But I was afraid and . . . I thought La Tejana Roja loved me!"

As she commenced to blubber up Longarm said soothingly, "Aw, don't cry, Miss Catalina. I'm sure Texas Red went on feeling tender to you as, say, a man visiting a sporting house still loves the wife at home. I know it's hard to understand, you still being a technical virgin and all, but what we call love with our hearts and what our private parts just got to have ain't always the same. As a . . . rider of the Owlhoot Trail, I've seen men and women get in trouble with sudden compulsions not even they were able to explain. I mean, how could anybody explain a man with a right pretty wife shooting his best friend when he caught him screwing their family dog? The house guest who abused his hospitality was a married man too!"

She giggled and said Inez had fucked more than one dog, and liked it. Then she said with a pout, "Is not just! I have turned down many chances for to be with a *muchacho,* and both Inez and *La Tejana Roja* have enjoyed the *vero todo*!"

To comfort her, Longarm let go of the spoon and took her in his arms to kiss first her brow, then her nose, and wind up with her tongue in his mouth as she grabbed his butt to thrust her pelvis up at him.

So they shoved the chili con carne on the back of the stove for now, and went into her handier room on the first floor to satisfy her hunger and curiosity about the real everything.

She was built more curvaciously than he'd expected when they got her shift off. He'd been comparing her in her duds to the bigger Texas Red.

She allowed that she'd never in her dreams imagined anything like he had to offer being offered to her that way, but gamely agreed to try, and as he parted her love lips with the throbbing head of his questing shaft, she decided it felt way better than the biggest candle she and Inez had ever "bent."

So Longarm satisfied her curiosity in many a position as they came more than once, before they got up and went out to the kitchen bare-ass to have supper seated at the worktable as innocent of duds as babes and feeling sort of like kids playing hooky.

After they'd eaten, Catalina took Longarm by the handle she liked best to lead him out to the front parlor and have a quick one on the leather chesterfield, laughing like hell. Then she got him to lay her on the carpet stairs, facing the front door, and they wound up in the bed he'd been sharing with Texas Red, where Catalina said she'd been introduced to the customs of the Isle of Lesbos.

As he pronged her in the same bed the old-fashioned way, she allowed that she might not be a natural Lesbos gal after all.

Having left his smokes and matches down in her room with his duds, he had to settle for just cuddling as they lay atop the covers fighting to get their wind back. His mind wandered some as the not-too-bright young thing prattled on about all the things she'd ever heard about sex, with some of them simply not practical. He saw now that he'd missed the chance to make a deal with Undersheriff Barrow. But then he reflected on what might have happened if he'd have been on that same northbound for a sort of awkward unexpected meeting with Texas Red, who hadn't said in her note whether she'd meant to leave town alone or not. A gal who kept two secret lovers from a man could as easily have more, and Longarm had noticed women who left one man almost always had another one lined up. It was against their nature to go it alone.

And he'd still been invited to the Galvez funeral on Sunday, and it wasn't as if he wouldn't have a roof over his head, an occupied bed under his sleepy ass, or grub in his gut until that Monday inquest. So it cut more ice to stay in bed with sweet little Catalina than to get up, get dressed, and pester Undersheriff Barrow at home after dark.

Dimly aware of what Catalina had just suggested in a drowsy tone with her lips bubbling on his bare shoulder, Longarm said, "Men ain't built like that, *querida*. A dirty-minded schoolmate told us all about female anatomy as we were shooting marbles one lazy afternoon back in West-by-God Virginia. I made more than one schoolmate of the female persuasion giggle like hell as I searched her in vain for that third hole he'd told us about."

Catalina didn't answer. She'd dozed off, Lord love her well-exercised ass. So, not wanting to disturb her and having no place better to go, he stared up in the gathering darkness to make some more serious plans about the future, once he was shed of that coroner's inquest.

He decided not to give away his true identity unless he was forced to. He had to still be Shadow Manners when he looked his old pal Skippy up in Wichita. Asking to be taken to the lair of a gang leader who'd see at first sight he wasn't the killer hired to shut Clem Aherne up would be dumb as hell. But he'd want to confirm that Sand Lachlan was indeed at the Dexter Hotel before he busted in with a raiding party, and with any luck, he might winkle a few other local addresses out of Skippy Steiner before he dropped the bullshit and reached for his six-gun and badge.

He fell asleep himself as he was composing another progress report sent in code at night-letter rates. So he wasn't aware he was dreaming when Texas Red laughed like a mean little kid and got into bed with him and Catalina. But when she went down on him, she started sucking too rough and he said, "Hey, watch them *teeth*, little suckerfish!"

She muttered in what sounded like Spanish with a mouthful, and it felt way better with her lips pursed over her teeth like so as Catalina was kissing him French on the lips. So he woke up all the way to see it was too dark to see exactly what Inez looked like as he pulled it out of her mouth with a pop and rolled her on her back to finish right, where they both wanted it.

He could tell she was way chunkier as well as way more experienced as she gave a swell ride to a man who'd had plenty of sleep, if Inez had seen Texas Red off at midnight and driven the buckboard all the way back to Alamogordo. She came just before him, and as he followed close behind, she sighed. "*Muchas gracias*. Has been some time since I have come like so, and by the way, I am called Inez Garcia Pedilla y Valdez."

Longarm said, "I know. Catalina here said we might be expecting you to join us."

Chapter 10

In point of fact, Inez had made it back a little after four in the morning to find his duds and six-gun in Catalina's room instead of her pal from the Isle of Lesbos. So she'd gone exploring with a candle. A *lit* candle this time, but she'd blown it out when she'd found the two of them fast asleep upstairs.

Her observation about his six-gun sent him downstairs, cussing his fool self, to carry everything back up to the bed of Texas Red. The fact that no members of Sand Lachlan's gang were in town didn't mean no other owl-hoot riders might not drop by a known hideout for hire!

Having secured their safety, Longarm got back in bed with the hired help, and by the time he'd satisfied Catalina in turn, it was getting light enough for a man to see what he was doing.

So he saw his Saturday in Alamogordo wasn't going to be a total waste after all. As she reclined like Miss Cleopatra to watch, the older but not bad-looking Inez had a somewhat paler hide covering way more ample curves. But her big old tits were still firm enough to inspire a man's admiration, and then it was his turn to watch as Catalina tried to help Inez catch up.

Longarm had discovered at other such times how two gals willing to go three in a tub usually liked one another too much to feel jealous. Gals who queered one another were inclined to be double-gaited as well as a tad more practical about such matters than men of any persuasion. For there were far more practical reasons for gals to indulge in such practices.

To begin with, women started out more tempted. Hardly anybody thought it queer for young gals to hug and kiss one another in public when they met up. So the feeling one was hugging forbidden flesh was less inclined to come up before it commenced to feel even better.

After that, gals were taking all sorts of chances men didn't have to worry about when they got down and dirty with total strangers. It was all too true some lizzy gals beat each other up, but a punch in the head from a 120-pound jealous lover was less likely to kill a gal than a roundhouse swing from a grown man, and of course, a gal letting herself go with another gal had fewer worries about some *other* accidents.

Most tempting of all, according to some double-gaited gals Longarm had talked to in the past, gals who wanted to be respected had to worry far more than men about their reputations. For a man said to like the ladies was inclined to be considered a sport, while a gal who screwed around was a slut. So lots of "old maids," living sedately together for year after year with nobody the wiser, got away with bare-ass slap-and-tickle that gents paid good money to watch in many a whorehouse.

Longarm found some of the girlish tricks Inez and Catalina played on each other while he rested up sort of awe-inspiring.

Like Catalina, Inez got a boot out of carrying on sassy all over the premises she'd been sweeping and dusting with her duds on. So as the day wore on, with spells of eating, smoking, and just chatting in between, Longarm wound up bedding one or the other in every room in the place. The gals were good sports about his having to move on before the new owners, and thus their new bosses, took possession come Monday.

Longarm suspected the new owners, by the name of Hogan in his field notes, had to know what sort of gals they were and what sort of boardinghouse Texas Red had really been running.

It was up to them if they wound up in jail by running the place the same way now.

He recorded other such places the law wasn't supposed to know about as old Inez turned out to be a font of information who liked to talk while she screwed.

She hadn't paid as much mind to Texas Red's instructions about the bedding of transient guests, and liked to brag on the famous gunfighters she'd bedded before him.

Longarm didn't care for such talk as a rule, but seeing it was his duty, he encouraged her to brag, and wound up with locations all up and down this stretch of the Tularosa Valley.

He didn't know if it would do any good to other lawmen now, but Inez confirmed Longarm's suspicion that they'd had Billy the Kid's part in that wild shoot-out at Blazer's Mill all wrong.

The reason there were so many versions of his part in the fight was that he hadn't been there. He'd been shot in the leg during the April Fools' Day ambush of Sheriff Brady and left behind, hiding out in the secret chamber under the bed of a Lincoln Plaza shopkeeper called Sam Corbett, and tended by Doc Taylor Ealy, while Dick Brewer led the others to that fatal meeting with Buckshot Roberts at Blazer's Mill on the eighth of April.

So if there was anything to her sensible-sounding tale,

not a one of the various versions of the battle at Blazer's Mill made sense.

For if Billy the Kid had been left behind in Lincoln Plaza with a shot-up leg on April Fools' Day, he could hardly have taken any part in the shoot-out with the small and crippled-up but mighty ferocious old Buckshot Roberts.

Blazer's Mill, owned by a retired dentist on the Mescalero Agency, was over forty miles by crow from Lincoln Plaza, or too hard a ride for any cuss who'd been shot in the thigh.

Longarm had heard others express the same opinion, that Brewer had led the Tunstall-McSween guns until he was killed at Blazer's Mill, with the Kid only getting so famous after the Lincoln County War ran down and he was still alive with a catchy nickname.

Inez gave him more certain stops on the Owlhoot Trail up north in Carrizozo, Santa Rosa, and of course Las Vegas. Not wanting to tip his hand, he didn't tell her how many lawmen knew Pete Maxwell's trail stop at Fort Sumner was used by all sorts of riders on both sides of the law, being so far from any county seat.

She told him how outlaws passing south through Alamogordo stopped next at Sunspot Springs, not Otero Grande as one might expect, if they were on horseback. Otherwise, she said, they stayed on the train as far south as El Paso. She said she hadn't heard it was that tough to sneak across the border lately. She agreed that Victorio sounded *muy malo* and advised "Shadow" not to make a break for Old Mexico just for being wanted for murder. So the gang that had stayed there recently with the cautious Lachlan had included at least one big blabbermouth.

By nightfall, the three of them could see their passionate menage à trois had wound down to showing off. So

85

Longarm got a good Saturday night's sleep, and a hearty Sunday morning breakfast after some wake-up slap-and-tickle with considerably calmed-down bedmates.

With the three of them searching through what was recently a boarding house, they managed a left-behind razor here, some shaving soap there, and wonder of wonders, one clean shirt out of four that fit him, even if it was Army blue instead of funeral white.

But Longarm still felt mighty awkward at the funeral of Pablo Galvez down the tracks at the old mission in the Mexican quarter. It wasn't as if he'd never been to a Mexican funeral before, and even if he hadn't, a well-traveled man with common sense and decent manners couldn't go far wrong if he just hung back a piece, watched what everyone else did, and went through the same motions.

The widow and her close kin were seated so far up front, Longarm felt sure they didn't know he was there in the back, near the entrance by the holy water font. There was no big deal about the way a stranger was supposed to behave around a holy water font. You just dipped two fingers in and made the sign of the cross. It didn't matter if you did it wrong, because nobody noticed unless you just stood there like the village idiot gawking at a public notice he couldn't read.

Longarm wasn't the only Anglo there. Some of the townsfolk, who'd come to pay their respects, being less well-traveled, acted more gawky as they mixed with Mexicans who hadn't been all that close with the Galvez family. So why was he feeling so out of place and unwelcome? They'd sent him a printed invitation, for Pete's sake.

But somebody there didn't cotton to him.

He wasn't catching any dirty looks. Rustic Mexican mestizo manners were tricker than that. Lots of trouble in the Southwest, going all the way back to the Alamo, had resulted from rustic Mexican manners and rustic Anglo manners being misunderstood by the other side. Good old boys only out to make friends could be accused of mortal insults, while Longarm had long since learned that, while angry *mujeres* were allowed to flash their eyes, a vaquero with Indian blood was never more likely to kill you than when he was smiling at you sort of shyly with his eyes sort of sleepy.

It was nobody's fault. Folks in different parts were raised different. Longarm had read somewhere how offering one of those North African goat herds a fine Havana cigar with your left hand instead of your right could inspire him to go home and get his gun, if he didn't stab you on the spot. Quill Indians who made white folks edgy by not answering when you spoke to them thought white fathers cowardly brutes for spanking their kids, and inhuman monsters when they refused to feed hungry Indian kids on credit.

As he watched the show from the back, having a tougher time following the padre's Latin than the Spanish it was related to, Longarm racked his brains for reasons more than one local Mexican might have for being sore at him. He didn't see how anybody outside the boardinghouse could know he'd been shoving it doggy-style to Inez while she'd been eating Catalina.

After the padre had jawed in Latin some, a friend of the family got up to pontificate in Spanish on what an *hombre vero* old Pablo in that closed coffin by the altar had been, giving up his life to save the honor of his *mujer* and all.

The penny dropped. Longarm knew what they were worried about. He held his peace through the service in the church. As they carried the coffin out, he fell in tight, removing his salvaged Stetson to the widow who'd been getting raped the first time he'd seen her.

She looked away. A younger Mexican with Apache eyes at war with some old Spanish ancestor's bushy black mustache edged between them to mutter in a murderous attempt at English, "My aunt does not wish for to ever speak to a gringo again! We know who you are. We know you finished off those others of your kind for my uncle. But they were still *chingados* of *your* kind and if I were you, I would be aboard the next train passing through!"

As they all filed out to the churchyard Longarm replied, "I sure would like that. As you likely know, I ain't from around here. But they won't let me leave before I back your aunt up on the way your uncle fought so brave for her honor against those saddle tramps."

Another husky Mexican walking ominously close to Longarm's back chimed in uncertainly, "You saw the fight? You were there when our aunt tells us Tio Pablo was hit from behind with a shovel, just as he was *winning*?"

Longarm shook his head easily and said, "Sorry to say, that other Anglo hand and me got there too late to back your uncle's play. We heard your aunt screaming for help and reined in. My pal held our ponies and so *he* didn't see *nothing*. I got there just as the raiders were making a break for it. Shot 'em both because they were headed my way with guns and neither looked like a woman who'd been screaming for help. What with the gunsmoke and dim lamplight, things were right confounding by the time I got inside. Your aunt was holding your poor brave uncle's head in her lap, too upset, like you just said, to talk to me. So my pal and me set some furniture back in place, hauled them dead drifters farther out in the dooryard, and just waited for the law."

He let that sink in before he added, "I'm pure sorry I can't offer a clearer picture of events out yonder. But you wouldn't want me offering details I wasn't certain of, would you?"

The one who'd as much as ordered him out of town smiled boyishly and decided, "Perhaps we have misjudged you, Señor Crawford. Is easy to see, now that we have spoken, you are an *hombre* who is not as quick as some of your kind for to run off at the mouth, and of course, the family is in your debt for coming to the aid of our poor aunt *just in time. Dios mio* knows what they might have done to a helpless woman if you had not saved her honor for our poor brave uncle!"

The one who'd been hovering within back-stabbing range moved around to fall in friendlier on Longarm's right as he invited Longarm home to supper after they buried Tio Pablo.

Knowing when to quit while he was ahead, Longarm said he'd been asked to sup with members of the local business establishment, and added in a confidential murmur, "It might be better, when I appear at the inquest to tell them how your uncle went down fighting, if it don't appear I'm a friend of his family, *comprende*?"

They did. But they included him in the family grouped closer to the open grave, and he was handed a dipper of dirt to scatter across the coffin as everybody filed past. He did so with respect, knowing it was an honor reserved for family and friends.

Somebody must have said something to the widow behind his back. For before he could get loose from the churchyard, she caught up with him to plant a motherly kiss on his cheek and softly murmur what sounded like one of those Irish blessings if she hadn't said it in Spanish.

So he went on back to the boardinghouse to spend his last night in Alamogordo if his luck held out. If they put the inquest off again, he'd have to flash his badge and let them hold it without the testimony of his mythical Crawford. For enough was enough, and that included Inez and Catalina.

So they parted friendly after an early-morning naked breakfast.

Then he unloaded the two old guns for twelve dollars, testified under oath with his fingers crossed at the coroner's inquest, and was free to barely make an afternoon combination north.

He'd figured that since he'd perforce been sworn in as somebody called Crawford, nobody knew yet who those rapists had been, and that seeing they were dead, it didn't matter what *else* they might have done after they'd killed old Pablo Galvez. The coroner's panel agreed they'd had a killing coming for killing an innocent man who was only trying his best to protect his wife's honor.

So as Longarm left, the records showed that Pablo Galvez *had*, with a little help from a passing stranger in the night, and for years to come folks passing through the churchyard down by the old mission would be pointing where a brave man lay moldering in his grave.

Longarm knew of many a bigger fib in recorded history.

Chapter 11

"Wichita" as such meant nothing sensible in any of the Great Plains dialects. Longarm figured it was likely a well-meant stab at "Wichasha," a Sioux-Hokan word meaning any grown man. He had it on the authority of many a "Wichita Indian" that the whole notion was *tachesli wasichun* or white folks' bullshit. *Wichasha* or *weya* meant man or woman and no more.

Down Mexico way, they'd wound up with the Yucatan Indians of Yucatan by asking Indians they grabbed who they were and what their hunting ground was called. "Yucatan" translated loosely from the Maya as, "What the hell are you talking about?"

But a rose by any other name would have smelled as strongly of boiled cabbage, coal smoke, horse shit, and steam as, thanks to having to transfer more than once, then wait spells on sidings while the highball combinations tore through, Longarm got in around nine in the morning, feeling seedy as the bottom of a canary cage and no doubt looking worse.

The store-bought tweed suit he'd left Denver in was a total disaster after all he'd put it through, and the fool newspapers kept running descriptions of his corpse some-where out yonder. So before he set up field headquarters right between the Dexter Hotel and Franco-Turkish Baths, Longarm made a few quick purchases after he wired Denver from the nearby telegraph office.

Then he booked a room with bath to sweat out Billy Vail's pick of the several choices Longarm had come with on his way north.

A body could sure come up with alternate plans while staring out into the dark aboard a pokey night train.

First things coming first, Longarm treated himself to a hot-tub soak and shave. Then he flopped, still damp and bare-ass, across the bedding to dry out in the cross-ventilation and maybe catch forty winks after such a pain-in-the-neck night sitting up.

But thanks to all the coffee he'd been killing time with, and no doubt to the stolen moments of sleep old soldiers manage without noticing, he was too keyed up to doze off. So he swung his bare feet to the braided rag rug and proceeded to turn into somebody else for local consumption.

He'd replaced both his missing Stetson and the hat he'd salvaged at the Galvez spread with the cheaper summer straw of the Kansas rural scene.

He'd treated himself to secondhand, although steam-cleaned, cavalry pants still bearing faded gold stripes down the blue-gray legs, and picked up a fresh shirt of Army blue to wear under a bolero jacket of new crisp-blue denim.

The State of Kansas had voted itself dry as far west as Wichita, and they'd frowned on packing guns in town when it was still possible to get lawfully drunk in Kansas. So, not wanting to explain his .44-40 over and over, he'd sprung for one of those shoulder holsters such as John Wesley Hardin had made so infamous and, sure enough, once you buttoned up the bottom of the jacket, the six-gun was riding out of human ken.

Unable to make any more important moves before he heard from his home office, Longarm circled the block the Western Union stood on to sort of get used to whatever anyone might take him for.

He studied his own reflection in a plate-glass shop window as he lit himself a smoke. The long, lean figure in mixed shades of blue and straw yellow didn't remind him of anybody that anybody was looking for. Those all-points wire broadcasts described a killer fleeing the D&RG wearing a prissy summerweight suit and a big Mexican sombrero while sadly asking all concerned to keep an eye out for a dead or dying lawman in tobacco tweed.

Longarm was still making up his mind about that tweed suit.

Had he had his druthers, he'd have never come by the infernal outfit in the first place. For while President Hayes and his First Lady, Lemonade Lucy, had done some good things by a country screwed, blued, and tattooed by the well-meaning but over-his-head U. S. Grant, their prissy dress code for federal agents hadn't been one of their better notions, and Longarm was inclined to work in more natural duds every chance he got.

So Longarm felt no call to have the travel-weary tweeds dry-cleaned and pressed there in Wichita. But knowing sooner or later he'd have to show up for work at the Denver Federal Building as prescribed by Lemonade Lucy, and seeing a new suit wouldn't look all that much better after he'd paid for it out of his own pocket, he decided to send the old suit by parcel post to his own hired digs in Denver with a couple of mothballs in each pocket for now.

He moved his less familiar-looking self to the board-walk across from the sort of high-toned Dexter Hotel as he stocked up on fresh cheroots at a corner tobacco shop. He wasn't sure why.

He had no idea what Sand Lachlan, Winks Malloy, or any of the gang save for Skippy Steiner might look like. So none of the faces moving in or out across the way meant toad turds to him. At the same time, old Skippy knew him on sight, and being hailed as Shadow Manners at easy pistol range could take fifty or more years off a man's life by giving the drop to a gang leader who distinctly recalled hiring another Shadow Manners on an earlier occasion.

Longarm cut back around the corner with the cheroot at a jaunty angle in his bared teeth. There had to be some way to get Skippy to point Sand out at some distance without making either suspicious.

There had to be some way to meet up with Miss Lillian Russell, spanking new in sassy comic operas and sassier on the cover of the *Illustrated Police Gazette* too, if only he could come up with one.

Meanwhile, he wasn't ready to make any moves before he got word on which approach he'd suggested met with Billy Vail's approval. So he ate an early noon dinner, and the next time he tried at Western Union, his crusty boss, Lord love him, had tossed some chips of his own in the pot.

Wording it the long way round, Vail told, or warned, Longarm he was about to stagger alive out of the Jornado del Muerto, saved by Digger Indians but needing some bed rest at Denver General and too exhausted to grant interviews to any but a few pet reporters he drank with, or slept with, in Denver.

Longarm had to grin sheepishly to himself as he wondered how the hell old Billy had found out about him and Miss Freedom Ford of the *Denver Daily Commonwealth*. But other than the invasion of privacy, old Billy's plan was likely to lull the cautious Sand Lachlan's uneasy feelings about a lawman with a rep on the tail of his hired gun.

The whole world knowing the one and original Longarm was laid up in a distant hospital bed would make it a whole lot easier to sell himself in Kansas as somebody else, as long as he didn't have to explain certain changes in appearance to the gang leader who'd hired the *real* Shadow Manners.

After providing more cover for Longarm, Vail thought their best bet would be to string Skippy Steiner along as far as possible, maybe even getting himself introduced to other gang members as the real hired gun until he had as many of them as possible located for, say, a four A.M. roundup by the local federal law. Billy didn't cotton to the notion of calling in the Wichita P.D., and Longarm followed his drift. He'd been the one who'd wired that there seemed to be a fair-sized outlaw network in the dry town of Wichita.

Making up some outlaw pals of his own he was staying with there in Wichita, so he could say he had other plans for that evening if he had to, Longarm ambled over to the Franco-Turkish Baths near the railroad depot. He could tell as soon as he entered the perfumed steamy interior that it was pure nancy-boy.

As late Victorians managed in an age of horsepower not to notice horseshit when they stepped in it, not to notice whores unless they rutted in the street or the dogs that *were* rutting in the street, they chose not to care what went on in "Turkish baths" as long as it went on inside in all that steam. So Longarm wasn't too surprised to be greeted at the desk out front by a muscular harem girl who needed a shave. The harem gal found Longarm more of a not-unpleasant surprise.

When Longarm said he'd come to scout up Skippy

Steiner, the harem girl said, "He's not in his digs upstairs at the moment. But I can always take half an hour off if you're feeling desperate, darling."

When Longarm said he wasn't there on that sort of business, the whatever-it was shrugged its muscular bare shoulder and said with a pout, "Oh, you're one of those crudies Skippy *rides* with, aren't you?"

When Longarm just smiled thinly, the harem girl said, "Your domesticated ape Winks had no call to punch me in the nose that time! What did Skippy tell you we were running here, a dirty old whorehouse?"

Longarm said, "I'll try again later. If Skippy shows up before then, I'd take it neighborly if you'd tell him Shadow Manners was in town."

The harem gal struck a pose and sniffed, "Skippy, Winks, and now Shadow? You're all so manly it makes a girl's mouth water. I suppose that as in the case of the ever-so-manly Winks, you never, ever, learned a word of Greek in prison?"

Longarm confided, "I don't know Winks Malloy that well. We are talking about a stumpy grumpy Irish-looking kid, right?"

The victim of Winks Malloy's earlier outrage frowned, not a pretty sight, and replied, "I don't see how we could be, darling. The ugly ape Skippy introduced as Winks Malloy was almost as tall as you, with a full beard going gray around the edges."

Longarm answered easily, "Oh, *him*? That's odd. I had him down as Honest Abe Jones. You're right about him being sort of tough to talk to."

He fished out his pocket watch and added, "Tell Skippy, when and if, I'll be back around four. He'll know why."

Then he ambled back to that tobacco shop across from the Dexter Hotel. In the darker interior, he found the same brown sparrow behind the counter. She chirped something about his earlier visit and asked what he'd forgotten to pick up.

Hoping he was right about how business had been so far that day, Longarm said, "I'll get right to the point, ma'am. I am a railroad detective, here on a delicate investigation I just can't tell you more than that about!"

She answered, "Oh, dear, I hope you don't think anyone working for me has been robbing any trains!"

Longarm chuckled dryly and confided, "Wichita P.D. vouches for your honesty, ma'am. That's how come I'm calling on you for some help. We aim to pay you for your time and trouble, of course."

Longarm had found in the past that offering money usually shut off the pesky questions. But the little brown gal of forty or so wanted to know what the Wichita police had told the railroad about her.

Longarm didn't have the least notion of the dear old thing's name. So he lightly told her, "Just that you'd been here a spell and hadn't robbed a train in living memory, ma'am. So here's the deal. I need to keep an eye on the hotel entrance across the way. I'm expecting a suspect on our list to scoot in and, with any luck, come back out with yet other faces I might or might not know at a distance. I don't want them to know I have that bottleneck covered. So I'm willing to bet you ten dollars you don't know how I ought to go about her."

The little sparrow came around the end of her counter to pull down the green canvas curtain of her shop's glass door and lock the door as she told him he had a lot to learn about the place.

Then she said, "Come with me. I live over the shop and my bedroom windows facing the street are hung with Irish lace. You'd be surprised by the things I've seen without being seen upstairs. That's quite a sporting crowd they have staying at the Dexter across the way, and some of them don't seem to know that just because you see white curtains in dark windows after business hours doesn't always mean nobody might be watching you and that painted hussy carry on!"

Longarm followed her up the dark narrow stairwell, feeling wry pity for a poor old gal living alone in a dry town. Folks could go queer in the head, jerking off in the dark as they watched less lonesome folks having a lot more action.

She said he could call her Lenore as she led him through her neat but cramped railroad flat the same width as her shop down yonder. He said that in that case his own pals called him Henry, and it served the tall drink of water who played that typewriter in his home office right. Longarm knew how unlikely it was that anybody would ever ask Miss Lenore who she'd led to those second-story windows across from the Dexter, but the less she recalled any names that mattered the better.

Leading him to the fresh-laundered lace curtains she'd mentioned down below, Lenore patted the nearby bed-covers and added, "I've found you can see a whole lot sitting up in bed with the lights out. So make yourself to home, Henry, seeing I'll be downstairs and we're both dressed proper and acting in the name of the law."

Longarm got out his wallet as he soberly agreed they were only doing what needed to be done. But then, as he handed over the ten dollars, he got a better look at the little brown sparrow who sold tobacco.

Facing him up close with the bright daylight through the white lace curtains hitting her smack in the pretty face, Miss Lenore was still in that chocolate-brown bodice that went so nice with her dark hair, but she was much closer to the softer side of thirty with her big brown eyes set in a heart-shaped face that would have looked natural on the pink pages of the *Police Gazette*.

She wasn't built bad either.

But Longarm was a good poker player, wasn't planning on staying there all that long, and so he managed not to grin like a shit-eating dog as he paid up and she left him alone in her bedroom, seated on her bedcovers, peering down through her lace curtains at the entrance of that fancy hotel across the way.

He was hoping Skippy Steiner, hearing his old pal Shadow was in town, would beeline to his gang leader for instructions before meeting up with a hired gun the gang owed money to.

Knowing what Skippy looked like, and pretty certain he'd be able to pick Winks Malloy out of a crowd, Longarm was hoping Skippy would come out across the way with Sand Lachlan, described on his yellow sheets as a muscular dapper dresser of medium height.

It figured that a halfway honest crook who owed a killer $250 would want to pay him off and send him on his way. It figured once Skippy and Sand Lachlan failed to meet their mutual pal at the Turkish baths, the gang leader, at least, would return to the hotel across the way. If things went that smoothly, Longarm had plenty of time to recruit some local raiders. If they went some other way, he'd have to play it that way.

The bedroom door behind him opened. He turned with a thin smile to see Miss Lenore standing there with a coffee tray. She told him, "I've closed for the day. I was going mad down there, wondering if I was missing anything, and of course, I knew you could probably do with some coffee, cake, and . . . company?"

Chapter 12

Miss Lenore set the tempting coffee tray on the bed by Longarm's rump, and took her own seat on the far side as Queen Victoria might well have suggested, seeing it was barely past high noon outside and they were out to catch crooks together with all their buttons buttoned.

Her coffee was Arbuckle brand, the pound cake and glazed doughnuts from the bakery just down the way were fresh-baked, and she'd thrown in a pack of his brand of smokes.

Then things got more awkward.

As a railroad dick called Henry, Longarm had never asked the pretty little sparrow bird's last name, marital status, or how she'd wound up owning and running her own tobacco shop in Kansas with that Tidewater, Virginia, accent. You could tell folks from the Tidewater, unless it was up Canada way, from the way they'd say "oot of the hoose" instead of "out of the house." Otherwise, both talked naturally enough, and Longarm didn't care. But Lenore Armstrong née Byrd was one of those gals it was best not to sit next to on a cross-country train if you didn't want to hear how they'd come West to seek their fortunes after their quality folks had been ruined by Reconstruction and they'd wound up married to a middle-aged but kindly and still mighty virile tobacconist.

Lenore told how she pined for her "Dear Old Bear" as she pressed more coffee and cake on her visitor. She explained how the Angel of Death had come for her Dear Old Bear as they'd been "holding hands" in that very bed. Then she hastily added that the late Angus Armstrong had finally breathed his last over at Sedgwick General after imitating a vegetable for a spell.

Longarm felt it might sound awkward to observe he was glad they were not sharing coffee and cake on a deathbed. He'd have cared way less if Lenore had really been the middle-aged nothing-much he'd first taken her for. But catching balls thrown his way by such a tempting bundle of fluff, and not tossing them back as hard, was distracting as all get-out, even if it did help pass the time.

Longarm knew he had to be back to the Franco-Turkish Baths around four whether anything interesting happened across the way or not. He'd left word he'd be there then, whether Skippy Steiner got his message or not. Riders of the Owlhoot Trail who left big fibs for their friends soon had no friends along the Owlhoot Trail.

So as Lenore was going on about some of the things she and her Dear Old Bear had seen across the way after dark and, well, been inspired to try some things they'd never learned in Sunday School, Longarm was working on what came next if he simply failed to contact the only member of the gang he knew for certain on sight.

Then, no later than quarter to one, things got to looking up as Skippy Steiner and some taller specimen Longarm didn't know came along the walk across the way to stop, shake, and part friendly out front of the Dexter Hotel. Skippy, wearing a sort of sissy seersucker suit and new Stetson with its high white crown creased Texas-style,

101

went on inside as his pal in darker summerweight gabardine and less wild and woolly hat went on to wherever.

His eyes glowing like those of a store cat staking out a mouse hole, Longarm was barely aware of the way his horny hostess had rambled on before she insisted, "Well, don't you?"

Honesty sometimes being the best policy with a woman you hadn't been listening to, Longarm replied, "You'll have to excuse my being distracted just now, ma'am. That squirt in the sissy suit and big bad Texas hat who just ducked into the Dexter is one of them train-robbing suspects I told you about. You were saying?"

She leaned closer to the lace curtains, asking, "Who? Where? You should have told me sooner!"

When Longarm failed to answer, she sighed and said, "I never see half what you dirty-minded boys spot first! I still don't see how Angus could have been so certain about where that traveling salesman across the way had it inside that colored chambermaid. But as I was asking just now, don't you agree with my Dear Old Bear that the State of Kansas had no call to pass unenforcable laws regarding what a man might or might not want to do with his very own wife?"

Longarm smiled thinly and replied, "Oh, *them* Kansas laws, Miss Lenore? Them sophisticated sodbusters in Topeka pass more laws than you can shake a stick at, and I fear they do pass some whizz-bangs. I like the one about the trains best."

She allowed that he had to know more about trains in Kansas than tobacco.

He said, "I've won bar bets in Kansas saloons that ain't supposed to be open in Kansas with Topeka's famous safety ordinance regarding cross-country railroad traffic."

He struck a pose to recite from memory. "Be it resolved that whenever steam locomotives find themselves

102

approaching, whether on single or double tracks, both locomotives shall come to a complete stop and neither shall
proceed before the other has safely passed."

She had to run that through her pretty little skull again
before she laughed uncertainly and decided, "That's impossible, you big silly! How could one hope to enforce
such a silly law?"

He shrugged and replied, "Same way they enforce the
prohibition against strong drink in trail towns like Dodge,
I reckon. The powers that be are forever passing laws that
few if any would want to see enforced. If I recall some
of those so-called crimes against nature your late husband
found so constraining the same way, I do agree with him.
For unless Topeka would care to stand a vice squad detective in every Kansas bedroom, posing as a lamp, I don't
see how you'd ever know for certain what grown-up and
responsible adults were up to round the clock."

She went into that old question whether infants had as
much fun at infancy as adults had at adultery. But Longarm wasn't listening. Skippy Steiner had just come out of
the hotel across the way with a burly bearded cuss around
forty-five or older. So he asked the gal who peddled
smokes right across from the Dexter if she knew him.

As the two gang members were shaking to part friendly
down yonder, the gal, peeking through her curtains with
Longarm, said, "Oh, that would be a Mr. Sullivan, I think
he said his name was. He's a growly old thing but polite
enough, and I'm one of the few tobacconists in this part
of town to stock those oddly scented Filipino cigars."

Longarm said, "Well, if it describes as a duck, shakes
hands with a duck for certain, and rooms in a hotel known
to be frequented by ducks, I'd say you'd just seen a duck,
and you say he smokes odd Filipino cigars, Miss Lenore?"

She replied without hesitation, "Magnolias de Manilla,
albeit they smell more like lemon rind and rosewater to

103

me. But who am I to argue when they sell for fifteen cents apiece and the growly thing buys them by the box?"

Longarm allowed he followed her drift as he consulted his fool watch some more to see he had over three hours to kill before he returned to the Franco-Turkish Baths.

She asked in a worried tone what he aimed to do next. He soberly told her, "Reckon I'd best stay put for now, ma'am. I could get on back to my own hotel if I'm making you edgy with my own bay rum."

She allowed she'd been enjoying the faint remnants of his aftershave lotion, and asked what made him think she might be feeling . . . edgy.

He truthfully replied, "Human nature, Miss Lenore. I don't want anybody on the other side to know where I am before I show up at a time and place I've led them to expect me. So I got to stay off the streets until well after three, and you know what they say about the Devil finding work for idle hands, don't you?"

She rose to set the coffee tray to one side before she turned her back to him, murmuring, "I do indeed, and I fear for the virtue of my own idle hands after dark if we allow this golden opportunity to slip away, Henry."

Longarm rose to the challenge, as most men would have, but even as he gingerly reached for her cloth-covered buttons, he felt obliged to warn such a friendly little gal, "I'll be pulling up stakes and moving on no later than three-thirty or, well, four at the latest. I might or might not be back this way sooner, later, or never, and . . ."

She stamped a foot and snapped, "Then let's get cracking, you shy old thing! Did you think I couldn't tell time? Do you think I don't know how little time we have and, oh, damn, let me do my own buttons, you big old butter fingers!"

So he let her, and she still beat him under the covers

in her breath-catching birthday suit, for she'd already gotten rid of all her underwear downstairs. And then they were having too much fun to talk about what they were doing to one another.

So once they had, more than once, Longarm got to hear how tough it was for a lusty young widow living across from a transient hotel to keep up appearances.

As they shared a dollar cigar propped up on pillows, Longarm declined her offer to show him how a widow woman who never messed with her customers could puff a big fat cigar with her other lips.

So Lenore showed him how she smoked something she liked better than tobacco cigars with her other lips. She called it holding hands because she kept one hand wrapped around most of the shaft to bob-bob-bob like a red, red robin choking on a gopher snake she'd taken for a worm.

Longarm had no complaints. Few men would have. But as he took luxurious drags on that expensive cigar while she took drags on him, he could see how the Angel of Death might have found it an easy chore to carry off a happily married-up older man subjected to such delightful violations of Kansas Statute Law.

Feeling nearly as pressed for time, Longarm helped her commit a mess of other so-called crimes against nature in the time they had to work with. She'd spotted some across the way that her Dear Old Bear had died too soon to try with her. Game for anything that didn't leave lasting scars, he was able to convince her that some of the whores she'd been peeping at had been showing off for customers. He told her about this Hindu book you bought from under the counter in a plain brown wrapper, and she said she and the late Angus Armstrong had tried in vain to get into some of those positions.

As he shoved it to her standing up against the floral

wallpaper, Longarm idly wondered if there was a married couple in all the land who'd never heard of the notorious *Kama Sutra,* or failed to pick up a copy.

By going on three they were both suffering rug burns and shortness of breath. So once he'd satisfied Lenore's curiosity about the Chinese Wheelbarrow position—she said it made her feel dizzy in the head—she didn't argue when he said he had to get it on over to that other meeting. She shook his limp dick with a game smile, and allowed that she felt sure he wasn't off to meet another woman anywhere else in town.

He'd had no call to tell her he was hoping to meet a bank robber in a nancy sweat house. He just got dressed, swore he'd never forget such a swell afternoon either, and strode on over to the Franco-Turkish Baths, walking a little less stiffly once he'd crossed a few streets.

When he got there, he found Skippy Steiner and that same gabardine suit and Texas hat waiting for him out front. Skippy introduced his other pal as a Percival he'd been showing the ropes, and suggested they repair to a chili parlor serving moonshine from the Indian Territory to the south.

Longarm didn't ask how they got away with it. They got away with that Long Branch Saloon in Dodge, and the Franco-Turkish Baths back yonder let clients in their own back rooms do things to one another the blue laws of Kansas didn't allow a man to do to his own wife.

Longarm was too polite to ask, and didn't really care, whether Skippy or his younger pal was the bride or groom as they tried not to let it show they were on their honeymoon.

Once the three of them were seated alone with a fifth of Maryland Rye and a scuttle of draft chasers, Longarm learned right off that his plan on a predawn raid on the Dexter Hotel was out of the question.

Not one member of the gang would be there.

For as Skippy explained, "You'd have missed me as well if you came in tomorrow. Our bunch has throwed in with others to pull a really big job up Wyoming way. We've all been tidying up our campsites so as not to be missed when none of us are here for a spell."

Longarm poured all around, since he'd paid with some of the money he'd gotten in Alamogordo for those antique weapons. As he did so, he quietly growled, "It's just as well I blew in today then. Sand Lachlan still owes me for old Clem and that lawman trying to get him back to Colorado."

Skippy said, "No, he don't. Longarm lived. Just read about that in the afternoon editions. But he's laid up in the hospital and we don't have to worry about him for a spell. Sand knows full well you still got two-fifty coming. He told me to let him know the minute you got to town. So when they told me about you scouting me up at the steam baths, me and Percival here got right over to the Dexter to let Sand know, see?"

Longarm saw why Skippy hadn't taken his nancy pal into the hotel. The local boy wasn't a member in good standing, and Skippy shouldn't have been spouting so freely about gang business in front of the sweet young thing. But it wasn't Longarm's problem. So what the hell.

He asked when he might expect his damned payoff for a job done well enough, God damn it.

Skippy said, "Don't get your bowels in an uproar, Shadow! I'd not have stayed behind to wait for you if Sand hadn't wanted you paid off."

Longarm asked, "Have you got my money?"

Skippy said, "Nope. We're waiting here for transportation. Sand left your payoff and travel expenses for me with a . . . business associate here in Wichita. Come sundown we'll be driven out to meet in confidence where the sun don't shine and the neighbors don't mind, see?"

Longarm snorted, "Seems like a heap of fuss for a lousy two hundred and fifty damn dollars."

Skippy nodded, explaining in a dismissive tone, "Sand's been under a lot of pressure, and of course the Dutch Uncle plays his cards so close to his vest that hardly anybody can say for certain what he looks like."

"You boys riding with Sand Lachlan are tied in with that mysterious *Dutch Uncle* nobody seems to know shit about?" asked Longarm, as Shadow, in a desperately casual tone.

Skippy said, "Sure we are. Didn't Sand tell you the Dutch Uncle was the architect when he robbed that Colorado bank the damned feds got so excited about?"

Longarm sipped some suds to mask his excitement. For the stakes in the already dangerous game had just gone up. A lot. Sand Lachlan was wanted as a cut-above-average bank robber. The professional criminal mastermind known only as the Dutch Uncle, if he really existed, was said to have had a finger in most every big robbery since the Northfield Raid.

Fans of the Dutch Uncle said Frank and Jesse would have pulled off that Northfield Raid had they let the Dutch Uncle set things up for them.

Chapter 13

Longarm had seen other natural blabbermouths rein themselves in when pressed to spill more beans. So he changed the subject by mentioning those old rifles he'd unloaded in Alamogordo, and asked if Skippy wanted to go on paying for their drinks or if it was time to settle up.

Skippy grumbled that he'd have asked twice as much off that gun-dealing Mexican rascal, pointing out, "That Winchester '66 sold new for more'n forty dollars and the Spencer was a fucking heirloom!"

Longarm said, "The Czar of All the Russians paid Smith & Wesson thirteen dollars a head for all them Special Order Army Schofields well this side of 1866, and you can still pick up a Russian Schofield in any hockshop for two bucks. I took what I could get. You want the cash left? Where's this fucking ride to wherever and the rest of my own fucking money?"

It worked. Skippy said, "Fuck the small change. I never paid for them old guns to begin with. The driver they'll be sending to pick us up after sundown feels safer in the dark. The way I understand it, we'll be run out to a hog farm on the edge of town to pick up what's due us. Then the same driver will run us back here and, should anyone ever ask, we might or might not be able to say just where that hog farm was, see?"

Longarm said, "Not hardly. I can see why old Sand might want to keep *me* in the dark here in Wichita. But you're a member of the fucking gang! Why couldn't he have just given you your money, left you with more to give to me, and been on his merry way?"

Longarm managed not to grin like a coyote in a hen-house when the one they'd left behind to tidy up confided, "Sand says he wants witnesses you got what was coming to you. I told you he was under pressure. Winks and a couple of the others have raised the question of them negotiable bonds from our big Colorado robbery. Sand says from now on he means to make dead certain everybody sees all the cards on the table faceup."

Longarm figured the real Shadow Manners would have had the right to know. So he asked, "What might Winks and the others be wondering about the loot from that earlier job?"

Skippy shrugged and said, "Where it's *at*, to begin with. When old Clem Aherne got testy about that down El Paso way, Sand said he'd feel safer by far if we all understood we'd never find out where he cached them bonds this side of the border when we couldn't get across it to cash 'em in."

Longarm, as Shadow, marveled aloud, "You boys let a man *live* when he refused to say just where all that valuable paper you'd ridden off with might *be*?"

Skippy said, "Hell, Shadow, you of all riders ought to know how old Sand gets his back up when you crowd him. They don't call him *Sand* because he's got no grit, and as Sand pointed out, it was Clem Aherne, not himself, starting arguments amongst ourselves as he, Sand, was

110

working to get us all away from the border with all those lawmen closing in, see?"

Longarm said he was commencing to see. He didn't consider it the time nor place to wonder aloud how come Clem Aherne had been first arrested and then assassinated after questioning the business practices of such a thoughtful leader.

As Longarm shifted his balance to suit the suddenly new footing under him, he could already see it seemed safe to push the charade way past the original plan. The only gang member who could say he wasn't the real Shadow Manners seemed to be off to Wyoming, with Skippy and even Percival yonder proud to introduce him as the good old boy who'd shot Clem Aherne to save their collective asses!

Better yet, with the bird they'd almost had in the hand off to another bush, Longarm and his true pals had their sights set on a really big-ass bird! Or they would as soon as Longarm could wire Denver there really was a Dutch Uncle after all.

The original term came from the newspaper game, where cub reporters ran their rough copy past older and wiser hands who knew the ropes way better.

"Dutch" was a catchall for things that weren't real. Dutch silver was an alloy with no silver in it. A man with Dutch courage was a fighting drunk. A Dutch fuck was what you got when you lit your smoke from the tip of a pal's cheroot, and so it went, with a Dutch uncle being somebody as smart as or smarter than any real uncle one might have had.

Longarm had heard of the Dutch Uncle along the Owlhoot Trail a year or more earlier. But this was the first evidence the son of a bitch might be more solid than the Will-o'-the-Wisp, the Fool Killer, or the Great Speckled Bird. So Longarm knew Billy Vail would expect him to stretch his luck and his neck a bit further down the pike.

Pretending not to think too much of the treacherous Sand Lachlan or his mysterious Dutch Uncle, Longarm backed the conversation up to where he and Skippy had split up in Alamogordo, and once he'd bragged some on his own adventures since, Skippy just had to sound off about all the wonders he'd seen and cucumbers he'd eaten up Wichita way.

Longarm knew Skippy was showing off for his new sweetheart as he went on about that Wyoming project. To encourage Skippy, Longarm acted as if he'd had enough to drink and didn't know a thing about Wyoming.

Skippy hauled his snout out of the suds to pontificate, "I been there more'n once, and Cheyenne's about as big as Wichita with nicer weather in high summer. They got this big old Greek temple made out of cast-iron near the depot with about the biggest taproom west of the Big Muddy, and it ain't but a spit and a holler from the fancy hotel we'll be staying in."

Then he corrected himself with a sly grin to add, "I mean me, Sand, and the boys. *You* two don't get to come along. Sand says he 'spects old Shadow here will head back for El Paso and, I'm sorry, Percy, I wasn't sure they were ready to hear about you and me just yet."

Percival sniffed and said, "I wouldn't know how to *begin* robbing a bank!"

As Longarm hoped, without any urging on his part, Skippy launched into a lecture on getting in and out while they were still shook up and not certain what you'd looked like or which way you went.

Thanks to his own experience with bank robberies, Longarm was able to volunteer some helpful hints few honest young cowboys would be expected to know about. He wanted Skippy dead certain he was introducing a fellow crook to anyone else they might meet up the Owlhoot Trail.

Longarm wasn't too clear, and didn't know how clear he wanted it, as prissy Percival dropped coy remarks from time to time. Longarm was able to guess the professional swish was more interested in Skippy's money at hand than plans for the future. It seemed "Shadow Manners" wasn't the only one there in line to be paid for past services rendered. When Percival made a snotty remark about an Army payroll and a railroad payroll passing through the same Cheyenne counting house sounding tougher to spend in Kansas than money *earned* in dammit Kansas, Skippy flared, "I told you we'd settle up afore I left and I meant it, sweet lips. You can come on along this evening, and once we part friendly with old Shadow here, we shall settle up indeed."

He grinned owlishly at Longarm to add in a roguish tone, "I'd offer one and all a swell party. But Shadow here is queer for women."

Percival softly sang a few bars of that old trail song that sort of went, "It's your misfortune, and none of my own, that from now on Wyoming will be your new home!"

Longarm was enough of a sport to join the laughter. But that was all he got out of either before one of the Mexicans from out front came back to tell them their ride was waiting.

Longarm had been trying to nurse his time-killing joy-juice, and he still felt it when he got to his feet. So Skippy and his sweetheart were walking even sillier as the three of them made it out into the gathering dusk, where another curtain side surrey waited at the curb behind matched black Friesians. The driver steadied the team afoot as the three of them got in, with the sweethearts in the backseat and Longarm up front with the Mexican driver. She seemed to find the three of them surprising too. As she got in to the left of Longarm, she said, "I was told I would be picking up no more than two of you."

When Skippy slurred, "Thash aright, Skinnyrita, we told old Percy he could come out and play with ush!" she stared thoughtfully at Longarm and said it was jake with her if he came along.

Longarm never corrected her as she snapped the ribbons and drove away from the center of town at a perky trot, cursing the bones of the two-headed dwarf who'd sired the driver of a beer dray as she cut it sweetly off with a snap of her buggy whip. He was more interested in who she was than he was in setting her straight about his more casual dress and way cheaper hat. Somebody, whether Sand Lachlan himself or his mysterious Dutch Uncle, seemed to favor innocent-looking young gals for sneaky buggy drivers. The still-shapely-if-she-watched-it brunette driving them wherever with imperious skill was what her own kind described as *sangre azul*, or white enough so you could see the blue veins in her wrists, and her wide-set feline eyes were blue as well. She had coal-black hair, eyebrows that met in the middle, and a faint but noticeable mustache. Having met up with her Spanish breed before, Longarm suspected she had a streak of black fuzz all the way down her spine to the mighty hairy crack of her ass. He idly wondered why he wondered about things like that. She was driving him to be paid off, not for her own physical examination, Lord love her hairy hide.

He knew what she'd think if he asked where on earth they might have met before. So he never did, and decided that Spanish blue bloods with eyebrows that met in the middle *all* looked as if you'd met them somewhere before.

It was a clear but moonless night, and once they were in the outskirts of town, one lamplit window to either side

114

looked much the same as any other. But the hairy little thing with the snappy whip and right nasty mouth, if you knew some Spanish, turned into a dooryard as if she'd been there in broad day, and as her three passengers got down in the tricky light, Longarm figured she had. She handed the ribbons to a dark form that loomed up out of nowhere, and directed the three to follow her toward a pinhole of light in the middle distance.

When they got there, a barn door slid open to spill more light for the time it took them to step inside. Then the door slid shut and a politely smiling but insistent rider all in black said they had to check their guns with him. He had a barrel handy, standing in the dust and chaff near the door. Skippy was the one who demanded to know what the fuck was going on. He pointed out he was a member in good standing of what he described for the first time as The Web.

A second politely firm gunslick explained, "Paymaster has a lot of cash in the back. We'll all feel safer if you boys check your guns out here for now. Please don't make me ask you again."

Longarm broke the ice by unbuckling his shoulder rig and handing over his .44-40. Skippy surrendered his Colt Lightning .38 with a remark about reporting all this chicken-shit higher up as soon as he got to Wyoming. Percival grudgingly surrendered a surprisingly lethal little whore pistol chambered .45-short as Skippy asked if he was allowed to keep his pants on.

The smoother-talking of the two by the door purred at them to follow him on back. So they did, with an undetermined number trailing them as Longarm tried to sort out the dusty footsteps in a long-deserted barn that held more echoes than hay in its loft up yonder.

They wound up near another barrel beside what looked to be a garbage pit dug into the dirt floor. Skippy recognized the heavyset cuss in a silver-trimmed black charro outfit as an old pal called Alejandro. When he said so, the Mexican coldly replied, "That was then. Where is the big sombrero they told me Manners here would be wearing?"

Skippy said, "Shit, we lost that dead giveaway before we made it to Alamogordo. What's this all about, Alejandro? Sand told me we were to meet you out this way after dark so's you could pay off Shadow here and fix me up with the train tickets and road expenses to Cheyenne."

Alejandro calmly replied, "Change of plans," as he produced his own Le Mat revolver, the only pistol chambered for both pistol and shotgun rounds.

Made in France by sullen brutes, the big horse pistol had its nine .41-caliber chambers wrapped around a core that was in essence a sawed-off .66-caliber shotgun. The nine pistol rounds came out single-action by way of the regular pistol barrel. The lethal blast of double-aught buck came out of a bigger muzzle beneath it.

Alejandro demonstrated exactly how his Le Mat worked by blowing poor old Percival off his feet with the shotgun shell before he swung the muzzle to put three rounds in Skippy before Skippy had figured out what had just happened to Percival.

Then Longarm was staring into the smoking over-and-under muzzles of the Mexican's Le Mat as Alejandro explained not unkindly, "Was only paid for to silence Shadow Manners and Skippy Steiner for because they knew too much. Skippy was told to bring only Manners there. But he chose for to bring you along, and now you too know too much."

He glanced down at the hole near his feet to softly add, "This hole is not big enough. We did not dig it for to hold *three* of you. Be a pal and dig it wider for us, eh?"

Then he called, "Ryan, give the nancy boy a shovel, *por favor.*"

Longarm had to laugh as he saw why he was still alive while Skippy and Percival were not. Sand had described Shadow Manners as tall and slender, wearing a suit under a Mexican sombrero. Nobody had told Alejandro to kill a tall, slender galoot wearing Army riding pants and a denim jacket under a Kansas farm boy's straw.

But the scene in the dimly lit barn got more serious as the one they called Ryan handed him a long-handled digging spade and muttered, "Get cracking, pansy! We ain't got all night for this bullshit!"

Longarm jumped down into the hole with the shovel as he held his palmed derringer between the shovel shaft and his sweating fist. He had just two shots to back his play, and there were four or more of them on all sides in the tricky light. Stalling for time, pretending to be the nancy boy they'd dismissed as harmless, Longarm asked mildly, even as he started to dig, whether Alejandro had considered how such a generous boss meant to pay him and his own boys off once they were done there.

Alejandro soberly replied, "Keep digging and let us worry about the future, *mariposa mia*. Is nothing personal, but you will not be there for to see how this all turns out."

Chapter 14

The hunter who says he's never suffered "buck fever" is admitting he hasn't done much hunting. And those who've suffered it know it doesn't feel at all the way it looks when you draw a bead, start to squeeze off a round, and . . . nothing happens.

There's no real fever. You feel fine. Your finger hasn't frozen solid on the trigger. You're free as ever to fire the rifle as you hold your aim, hold your aim, hold your aim, until the buck just ambles out of range and you wonder, "What the hell just happened?"

What happened is that you held your fire, knowing once you fired you were committed once and for all to hit or miss. So you held your aim and held it some more until it was just too late to fire.

As Longarm widened what he knew would be his grave if he didn't dammit make his move, he wryly understood why he was finding it so tough to let go of the damned shovel and do some damned shooting. He had to do what he had to do before they decided the hole would do. But he had two shots and two shots alone to work with, while there were four of them he could keep track of as he dug, with Lord only knows how many others back from the light a piece!

Throwing down on Alejandro wasn't going to get him out of the hole alive. But he'd at least take Alejandro and maybe another with him, and the one called Ryan was closer, to his right, so what the hell, maybe on the count of three, and then he'd counted to four and Alejandro had asked Ryan, "What you think? Is wide enough?"

Longarm's buck fever broke. But even as he let go of the shovel to throw down on Alejandro a woman screamed in Spanish for him to duck!

So he pegged a shot at Alejandro and dropped to the bottom of the pit with his own shoulder rig and holstered .44-40 while all hell busted loose in the cavernous barn.

Longarm let go of the derringer and shoulder rig as he drew the double-action six-gun without the least notion what in thunder was going on. So he kept his head down until the fusillade of rapid fire faded away and a familiar voice called out, *"Vamonos, Brazo Largo!"*

So he gathered up his shit, jumped out of that hole, and they got the hell out of there.

As she drove lickety-split through the dark, trusting the night vision of a racing team, she said she was called Yolanda. They both knew who he was, although El Brazo Largo, as "The Long Arm" came out in Spanish, did not appear on any records the U.S. Government approved of.

As El Brazo Largo he was wanted bad south of the border. For no matter how often he tried to explain his position to the fool Mexicans, both the self-styled government of Old Mexico and the majority of Mexicans opposed to a brutal dictatorship kept insisting Longarm was the sworn enemy of their Presidente Porfirio Diaz, bless his perfumed and powdered hide.

So asking a Mexican outlaw gal why she'd stuck her neck our for him back yonder would have been as dumb

119

as asking whether she spoke Spanish. If there was one thing most Mexicans without government jobs agreed on, it had to be that anyone wanted by Mexico was a true friend of Mexico, and the distinctions between Mexican patriots and Mexican outlaws had grown mighty fuzzy since old Diaz and his bunch had stolen the Mexican Revolution the late Benito Juarez had commenced with different goals in mind.

He couldn't see the Mexican spitfire who'd just saved his ass while they sped through a swirling confusion of blackness punctuated by flashes of lamplight and the barking of dogs. So his answer was sincere when she teased that he'd forgotten her and he had to confess she was right on the money.

She reined her team to a walk as they approached a line of street lamps across their bows and decided, "We are far enough from that grave you were digging for yourself, Brazo Largo. Would be more better if no *soldado chingado* asked for why we were driving so fast, eh?"

Longarm nodded soberly and replied, "Let's not worry about any fucking soldiers, Miss Yolanda! What about the outlaw gang you just shot up, *muchas gracias*? How will you ever justify that to . . . who were you working for until just now?"

She said, "Myself. Alejandro Duran was a how-you-say gun for hire I had known long ago in Chihuahua, when my husband was alive and in the business of moving livestock without formalities. When Alejandro heard I was dealing in . . . used merchandise up this way, he hired my services for to pick you and those other *pobrecitos* up for him. He said nothing about killing anybody. I would have said nothing about recognizing El Brazo Largo if Alejandro had not decided to kill a hero of *La Causa* in front of my eyes. I hope I have not, how you say, fucked things up for you. I saw no other way how for to save you. But now will be *impossible* for to go on pretending to be a *mariposa* in their eyes, no?"

Longarm smiled thinly and explained, "I wasn't trying to pass for the pansy. They took him for the other cuss I was trying to pass for. I might be able to turn what just happened to my own advantage if you can get me to the Western Union before what really happened gets transcribed into newspaper type from tonight's police blotter."

So she drove to the Western Union near his hotel, and he wired a coded message to Billy Vail at nickel-a-word day-rates and paid extra for home delivery, knowing old Billy would get it well before bedtime and that once he had, he could pull strings harder from Denver than anybody Longarm knew in Wichita. So now all Longarm had to do involved lying doggo until he saw which way the morning papers might blow.

He'd questioned Yolanda tightly on how many neighbors might or might not tie her in with Alejandro's bunch. He figured she knew what she was talking about when she said the neighbors on her side of the tracks never stuck their noses into anything without an invitation.

Once he'd wired his boss, Yolanda wanted to know where he wanted to go next. It was a good question.

He said, "I don't have anything of value in my hired room, and I don't want any hotel clerks saying they saw me alive in this part of town when the newspapers are going to report Skippy and his old pal Shadow dead in that barn. So I'd best hole up for the night somewheres else."

Before he could mention Lenore's tobacco shop, Yolanda said, "You got a place for to hole up if sick cats do not upset you. Nobody else will bother us at my place. Hardly anybody knows I live in the back of my pawnshop. But both my cats are most sick and I fear they do not smell so good."

As they pulled away from the Western Union, she added, "If I let them out at night I would think somebody had poisoned them. First my Tomas and then his *esposa*, Tina, throw up shit and shit vomit, and now they refuse for to drink water. But I have had them since they were *gatitos*, and I beg you not to order me for to kill them!"

To which he could only reply, "I hardly ever murder cats, even when they don't belong to friends, Miss Yolanda. You were fixing to tell me how come you recognized me back yonder, weren't you?"

She dimpled sideways at him as they drove east in line with the rail yards and said, "Long ago and far away was a *paseo* in my village of San Mateo. I was walking clockwise around the plaza with my good friend Ramona. You, of course, was strolling counterclockwise with the other *hombres*. The third time we passed one another Ramona smiled at you, and the next time we passed you smiled back, and I have never forgiven that *puta* Ramona!"

The penny dropped. Longarm laughed and asked, "Was that you with old Ramona at that *paseo*? I make no apologies, Miss Yolanda, for unless my memory fails me entire, I must have been blind drunk that night if I went home with anybody else!"

She smugly replied, "I was the one you asked first. You gave up when I told you I was married. How was I to know the famous El Brazo Largo was so shy? *Pero* no matter. Was a long time ago, and the last time I saw our Ramona she had become most fat!"

So he got to flatter her for her swell shape without suggesting a shave might not hurt. And by the time he'd stolen a kiss and some feels while they left her surrey and team at the livery down the block from her pawnshop, she'd forgiven him for all the bragging that other rebel gal had felt entitled to after no more than a one-night

122

stand with the notorious *yanqui* who'd shot those *rurales chingados* on their own side of the border.

Then they were back in her quarters behind the pawn-shop, and Longarm was sure starting to miss old Lenore's tobacco shop. For as a country boy Longarm had been raised to feel livestock belonged outside at night, and *healthy* cats at close quarters were about as much cat as he could take as a rule!

But rules were made to be set aside, and Longarm felt sincerly sorry when Yolanda hauled old Tomas out from under her bed, stone dead as well as mighty stinky.

As Yolanda found the calico Tina alive if not well under a sofa, Longarm sniffed more certainly and asked, "Have you been sharing *chocolate* with your pets, Miss Yolanda?"

She confessed she liked chocolate, but didn't want to eat whole boxes of it alone lest she wind up fat as old Ramona. So Longarm said, "There you go. You were right about your cats being poisoned, Miss Yolanda. Didn't anybody ever tell you neither cats nor dogs taste sweets? As born meat-eaters, neither species ever evolved to taste sugar. Albeit some hold *foxes* may taste sweets, the way they're forever nibbling grapes off the vine."

Holding the sick Tina in her lap as they both sat on the sofa, Yolanda replied with a mighty serious frown that met in the middle, *"Es verdad?* They both seemed to enjoy the treats when I shared my chocolate with them more than once."

He explained, "Cats and dogs smell and taste the but-terfat chocolate's made with. But there's this stimulant related to *cafeina* folks and dogs only feel as a little boost. But if there's one thing a born tensed-up and high-strung *cat* don't need, it's a *stimulant!*"

He reached out to casually pet her pussy as he added,

"This vet I know says the kick in chocolate hits cats like *cocaina*, and you've seen how drunk they can get on a harmless weed we call catnip. I disremember what you call it in Spanish. So, in sum, should the poor critter make it through the night, don't ever feed her chocolate again."

Yolanda asked what they could do for the *pobricita*.

Longarm soberly replied, "Nothing. It's too late to pump her stomach if we had the gear. She's eliminated a lot of it on her own, judging by the chocolate-scented fumes back here. If you can't get her to drink water, she's got enough in her system to last her or she ain't. The shakes she's suffering are inspired by her nerves telling her to lie down and run in circles on the ceiling at the same time. Do you mind if I open a window, Miss Yolanda? She looks like she's about to puke some more."

The sick cat's upset owner didn't seem to want a lap full of vomit, so she put Tina back in that closet and rustled up a carboard box for the remains of Tomas, while Longarm opened a sash window by her back door top and bottom. He saw she had burglar bars fitted just outside. Living through a house fire could be less of a problem than an armed break-in when you ran a no-questions-cash-on-the-barrelhead so-called pawnshop out front. Although, having seen Yolanda in action, Longarm felt break-in boys might be well advised to steer clear of her.

Yolanda seemed more sentimental about house pets than hired assassins who'd been unwise enough to hire her.

She made coffee to go with some chocolate cake, served off a low coffee table in front of the sofa, and it hardly seemed fair to fat old Ramona down Chihuahua way how a sweet tooth hadn't resulted in as much as one double chin so far, and by the time they'd consumed enough chocolate to kill another team of cats, the sickly-sweet smell of the two she'd managed to poison so far had either faded considerably, or else he'd gotten used to it. He felt no call to mention the funny looks he'd gotten in that high-toned hotel lobby after unwashed months in the saddle on the old Chisholm Trail. When he tried to tell Yolanda to just let her Tina be, she went to have a look anyway and came back to the sofa crying.

He didn't ask if old Tina was dead too when Yolanda blubbered how ashamed she was of her own stupidity.

She said, "I can judge to within the dollar what I might buy or sell in silver, gold, or precious stones. For why have I always been so *dificil* with *living* things I cherish?"

He'd already set his hat and bolero jacket aside. But he was still wearing his shoulder-holstered six-gun as he casually draped an arm around the back of the sofa to haul her closer, saying, "It wasn't nobody's fault. Miss Yolanda. You're a dealer in stolen goods, not a *veterinario* for land's sake."

She said, "Hold me closer *por favor*. As I said, I had the two of them since both were *gatitos,* but I do not feel so very very *solitario* with your so strong *brazo* around me!"

So he hugged her closer, and they naturally wound up swapping spit on her sofa for a spell. But as one feel followed the other as naturally as night the day, she shyly suggested she'd feel more comfortable in the dark, in her bed, if he really wanted for to take her clothes off.

So he picked her up to carry her off to bed, giggling some, and he got just a glimpse of her blue-blooded hide before she'd snuffed her bedside lamp, and decided it was just as well she had.

For her shapely naked body felt female as all get-out in his bare arms, and there was no mistaking her for anything but a gal as he entered her with a mutual hiss of pure pleasure.

But judging just by feel alone, she was hairer than him,

and it sure felt odd to have her firm but hairy tits pressed to his own hairy chest as she kissed him and called him her *querido mio* while she acted in such an otherwise womanly way.

Once he'd gotten used to her unusually fuzzy hide, he found she was as anxious as most gals who'd been living alone a spell to try some odd positions before agreeing, as usual, that the old-time fornication was good enough for their grandfolks and good enough for them.

So he was just as glad he hadn't gone back to old Lenore's place after all, and the both of them having had a long day, they wound up sleeping sound as babes in each other's arms.

For a spell leastways. But when Longarm woke up after sunrise, he saw Yolanda was serving his breakfast in bed with her own bare body hidden by a fuzzy navy-blue robe.

He didn't ask how come. Lots of things in an imperfect world looked better when you never looked at them too close.

Peel the hair and hide off Miss Ellen Terry and she'd doubtless look just awful.

Chapter 15

Yolanda had the morning paper delivered out front by a neighborhood kid. So once Longarm had planted the two cats out back beneath a rambler rose she said they'd liked to dig under, he searched the paper in vain for news of all that gunplay out at the hog farm.

If Yolanda was right about it having been a vacant property up for sale for some time, due to hog cholera having put the former owners out of business, it seemed possible Kansas law might first learn about the mess they'd left out yonder from Colorado law.

Yolanda knew at least a little about a lot of things around Wichita, and when Longarm decided she was just the best thing he'd stumbled over since he'd jumped off that train in the Jornado del Muerto, he wasn't just thinking about her fuzzy frisky flesh.

She was the first crook willing to work with him that he could level with, seeing she already knew he couldn't be up to anything crooked. It was well known down Mexico way that when he wasn't fighting *los rurales,* the famous El Brazo Largo was a famous *yanqui* lawman.

Being a born Mexican rebel of the female persuasion,

Yolanda had been raised to just go along with anybody opposed to Mexico City without too many questions, and Longarm had come to similar conclusions about Mexican rebels, on either side of the border, as long as they weren't breaking any *federal* laws worth mention. So she knew what he was and he knew what she was, and now he seemed to be *getting* somewhere!

From time to time that morning, a bell over her front door would jingle and she'd duck through the curtains at one end of her parlor to cope with customers from behind a sort of bank teller's cage with a double-barrel Greener twelve-gauge under the till.

Everybody who came in that morning had something to "pawn" as Yolanda wrote the transaction up. She "loaned" roughly ten percent of what she might sell anything worth selling for. She told one kid who came in to see if he could pawn a friendly Irish setter who'd followed him home not to bother her. But she let a housemaid hock some quality jewelry for thirty-five dollars, and never asked how a housemaid drawing a dollar a week might have come by anything worth three or four hundred used.

Longarm already knew. But Yolanda explained that customers buying anything at a pawnshop expected to pay no more than a third of its retail value new.

Business being slow that morning, and Yolanda unwilling to undress in broad-ass daylight, Longarm pumped her for current criminal news with an arm around her shoulders and one of her hairy legs draped over his cavalry pants. She knew she had nothing to hide from U.S. federal law, and thanks to her position, serving riders of the Owlhoot Trail without being usually required to *ride* the Owlhoot Trail, she knew as much or more about its Kansas network than many a more serious crook who'd *chosen* to ride it.

She was still pissed at the late Alejandro Duran and his bunch for the way she'd had her arm twisted to take part in a killing. When she'd tried to tell them she wasn't in that end of the business, Alejandro had shrugged, said she had that surrey, he needed her for to drive that surrey, and how did she feel about *la ley yanquis* asking questions about the big silver-mounted show saddle or that swell Italian violin she had for sale in her window. But when Longarm said he was mighty glad she'd been there, she fumbled for his fly and allowed she'd take him up on that.

As she rolled off the sofa to kneel between his boots, spread wide on her rug, he saw she didn't have to slip out of her robe to play tunes on the French horn. But Longarm had been raised to waste not and want not.

So as she was trumpeting him down the home stretch for the finish line between her tonsils, Longarm spread her like a fuzzy bearskin atop the rug that was already there, to finish in her right with his cavalry pants around his booted ankles, his Army blue shirt open down the front with her exposed hairy tits pressed to his heaving bare chest.

Yolanda sobbed, "*Ay, Dios mio, tu eres un vero locomotura!*"

But of course, once they'd died together, as poetic Spanish speakers put it, Yolanda wrapped her robe around her tight and would have crawled under the sofa if her curves had let her.

Longarm finished undressing as he sat bare-ass on the rug beside her. When he casually asked what had inspired all the weeping and wailing, she sobbed, "You have *seen* me, all of me, naked by the light of day!"

Fumbling in his discarded shirt for a smoke, he lightly replied, "You've seen as much of me, *querida*, but do you hear me bawling about it? Getting naked is the best way to go about it, and soon as I get my second wind, I mean to go about it some more. For you sure screw swell, you pretty little thing!"

She calmed some and asked in a wary tone, "You still say I am *bonita* after you see I am hairy as a man?"

He thumbed a light and got his cheroot going before he mildly replied, "No you ain't, no offense. I ain't one for bragging, but I got twice as much hair on my chest than I've seen on your own so far."

She laughed weakly and protested, "Is not the same! You are *muy hombre* and a big hairy *gringo* as well!"

He exhaled as he put the smoke to her pouty lips and suggested, "You must be part *gringo* then. I know none of you blue blooded *blancos* care to admit your blue blood ain't hundred proof all the way back to them painted caves where you say art was invented. Greeks keep assuring me *they* are the one poor race that never mixed with nobody else. And the history books say you're both full of fairy dust. Leaving the Greeks and the Turks to sort things out, the Iberian cul de sac at the west end of Europe's been invaded, and settled, by most every breed on Earth with the possible exception of Australian bushmen, and I wouldn't bet the farm on *that*!"

He took the smoke back, adding, "You may be a Viking princess who came out brunette. I met this Swedish gal working as a bearded lady for old P.T. Barnum, but that's another story."

Yolanda laughed like hell, allowed that if he didn't mind, she didn't mind, and hauled him back to bed with her. So the morning hours slipped past faster than they might have, and if it looked like he was exploring a briar patch with his dong as he did her dog-style, things felt just fine on the far side.

From time to time that distant bell would jingle, and she'd slip on her robe to duck out front and deal in stolen goods.

Between times, she intimated that some of the stuff folks wanted to hock out front could have been come by honestly. He warned her not to lose touch with the rules of the game she was playing just because he didn't approve of it. Helping her out of her robe again after a transaction, he told her not unkindly, "Miss Yolanda, I'm a lawman and you're a crook. You're a pretty crook and I owe you. But let us not be serving heaping plates of *mierditas* to one another just because we're pals. For as I have told more than one thief I've had to run in, I have more respect for a thief who knows he's a thief and doesn't try to sugarcoat it with remarks about *swiping* watermelons or *lifting* horses. Kids kidding one another about the terminology of, say, breaking and entering are the kids who wind up in jail before anybody else."

So Yolanda kissed him some more and promised to be bad if he really thought she was pretty. Then she got up and made them a swell noon dinner, naked as a jay in all her fuzzy glory.

Yolanda didn't have the afternoon editions delivered. So after they'd enjoyed a French lesson with their dessert, he got dressed and went out the shop door, hoping to be taken for a customer by anybody nosy enough to care. He saw he'd made the right move when a rider under a Texas-crowned Stetson coming along the plank walk said, "Howdy, Kansas boy. Mind if I ask a question?"

To which Longarm felt obliged to reply, "You call me a *boy* again and you'd best be fast on your feet as you are with your mouth, Tex."

Since all born bullies old enough to vote have learned to crawfish if the occasion should arise, the stranger grinned like a kid caught with his hand in the cookie jar and said, "Jee-zusss! I heard you Kansas Jay Hawkers could be touchy, but you sure must not be getting any lately. I was only out to ask, seeing you just come out of

131

that hockshop, whether you felt you'd been treated fair. I heard tell the place is run by this greaser gal who drives a hard bargain."

Longarm honestly replied, "Miss Yolanda's done me just fine so far. What might you have to hock, Tex?"

The stranger said, "Nothing. I'm buying, if she's got a double-action Colt or S&W chambered for .45-28's for sale at a fair price."

Longarm said he'd noticed some pistols hanging in the window back yonder. It wouldn't have been polite to ask a total stranger why he needed the preferred weapon of your average bank robber.

The Texas road agent or whatever allowed he'd just go on in and see for himself. Longarm strode on, committing the overall appearance of a possible want to memory with good reason.

The Army Springfield rifle was chambered .44-70 with shooting Indians for keeps in mind. The designation meant a .44-caliber bullet got pushed hard and fast by 70 grains of powder. The Army's .45-28 *pistol* round was meant to make recruits feel armed and dangerous without alarming them. A schoolmarm could handle the half-ass kick of 28 grains of powder, and if the bullet left the muzzle going barely faster than a kid with a slingshot could match, it was a big fat bullet and it did make a big hole in a cuss. So folks staring down the barrel of any gun with nearly a half-inch bore tended to do as they were told.

After that the nice thing about the puny Army pistol round, from the standpoint of a hold-up man, was that you wound up with less smoke in your way and your stray shots could be trusted to stay in the same room with you and your gun.

But had that waddie been serious about a side arm, he'd have been in the market for at least forty grains of powder or nigh twice the punch of the S&W Army Short.

Like most working-class Papist neighborhoods in a mostly Protestant West, Yolanda's was inhabited by Irish, Mexican, Polish, and Italian folks in about that order. The railroads, wanting peace and quiet as well as cheap labor, built colored subdivisions in enclaves along the tracks.

Longarm picked up an afternoon extra edition a block up the way, and not wanting to barge in on that Texas hat, scouted up a sidewalk *cafetin,* where he got to spread the paper out across the robin's-egg-blue table with his coffee and *tapas* or pastry surprises.

Longarm saw at a glance that good old Billy Vail had outdone his fool self, however he'd worded his wires to the Wichita District Court.

For a man who laughed at the airs of Buffalo Bill Cody, old Billy could write wilder Western yarns than Ned Buntline and Johnny Clum together!

Old Billy and young Henry out on the typewriter both enjoyed tracking wants through the files and they were both good at it. But Longarm could see, as he noted the colorful names and long records lifted from the yellow sheets across creation, how Billy had enlisted the help, or creative imaginations, of some Kansas as well as Texas pals.

In any event, it seemed the notorious Simon or Shadow Manners of border-town notoriety, suspected as the shootist who'd murdered the late Clem Aherne and hospitalized the famous Longarm aboard the D&RG, had died along with the possibly meaner Alejandro Duran, known to have killed men, women, children, pigs, and chickens at affordable prices.

Longarm wasn't surprised to read how Duran had been trained as a Mexican *rurale,* or ranger, and made it to patrol leader before he'd been drummed *out* of the brutal *rurales* for raping not the usual peon's daughter, but the wife of his commanding officer.

Local and federal law alike were still working on what the late Skippy Steiner had been doing out yonder or which side he'd been on in the fight. For witnesses had placed Steiner in the company of both notorious hired guns within weeks leading up to their fatal showdown in a vacant barn neither had asked permission to enter.

With the sweat-bath punk nobody seemed to be missing listed as Shadow Manners, the other four bodies out yonder had been written off for now as long-suspected if never-proven hard cases Alejandro Duran or maybe Shadow Manners had brought along to the showdown. The Wichita P.D. had two or more sets of footprints across the dirt floor than they could match with the boots of the seven cadavers scattered across all the dry dirt around an empty pit that the law was still trying to figure out.

Finishing the article and folding the paper away for Yolanda, Longarm paid up and drifted back, hoping he wouldn't have to explain how come to that bigmouth with the big hat.

He didn't. Yolanda said the Texan had left better than twenty minutes back with two dollars worth of hardware. When she recalled the caliber as .32, Longarm snorted, "He's fixing to get his fool self stomped and thrown in jail, if he's lucky. Many a grown man out our way considers it a mortal insult when you try to scare him with a .32!"

Yolanda said she never concerned herself with what clients might or might not want to do with anything she had to offer, from violins to cross-cut timber saws. So they went back to her bedroom to get undressed and go over that afternoon extra some more. Yolanda needed help with some of the longer words in English. She wasn't the first foreign gal he'd met who'd complained English spelling made no sense. It made the self-educated Longarm feel better about the spelling grades he'd earned in school before they'd given that war in his honor and he hadn't had to go to school no more.

Once she had the heavily edited account of their gunplay the night before figured out, Yolanda decided, "You would seem for to be in the clear, *querido mio*. This Sand Lachlan who prefers for to pay his hired assassins with assassination surely thinks you have been assassinated, no?"

Longarm shrugged and said, "He thinks I'm laid up in a hospital, and he just had the real Shadow Manners killed, along with the real Skippy Steiner. But he never paid them off with hot lead to save the two-fifty he still owed on Clem Aherne. Alejandro Duran would have asked the going price just for gunning Skippy. He'd have asked more to gun a man with the rep and the established skills of Shadow Manners. That's what old Alejandro was doing with that oversized Le Mat out yonder, see?"

She nodded and said, "Is easy for to see. If you were not working for such a teller of tales, this Sand Lachlan's worries would be over for all time. The captured comrade who might have talked is no more. The assassin hired for to kill him was just killed by Alejando Duran, along with the one surviving member of the gang with direct knowledge of the shooting and daring escape out in El Jornado del Muerto. This Sand Lachlan is on his way for to rob more banks, snug as the bug in that rug, he thinks, because with even Alejandro Duran dead, there is no way for to tie him in to that earlier robbery and so much double-dealing!"

To which Longarm replied with a wolfish smile, "Oh, I wouldn't know about that, *querida*. Billy Vail and me were racking our brains trying to figure how I'd get further up the chain of command than poor Skippy Steiner, and look how Sand Lachlan just dropped his pants for us and bent over to pick up the soap!"

Chapter 16

The trouble with playing with small fry you weren't fixing to reel in was that, as many a lawman had found out the hard way, he could get to treating shady informants as confidants, and so even as he rolled a nipple between thumb and forefinger, Longarm figured he'd said too much already. So when Yolanda asked what the two of them were fixing to do to the bent-over Sand Lachlan, he crawfished with, "Ain't certain what *I* aim to do, sweetheart. You've done more than enough by killing off Skippy, Shadow, and the last trigger man on Lachlan's side to see them alive."

She said with a pout, "*Eso es una mierda.* I never shot the two *hombres* with you. I shot Duran for because he had shot them and meant for to shoot you!"

Longarm said, "That ain't the way surviving gang members are going to read it in the papers." And then, catching his mouth going faster than a good fisherman played a shark sucker, he shut his own fool mouth with her turgid nipple as he slid his free hand down her hairy belly to feel for pussy astray in her briar patch.

It worked. She didn't ask how he planned to move in

on the gang now. She asked him to go easy on hitting bottom until just before they were to die together some more. So like many a shark sucker before her, Yolanda would never know exactly how the law had hooked a particular shark as she and others like her just scouted for other sharks to swim with.

There would always be other sharks, and hangers-on like Yolanda, Texas Red, et al to feed on the scraps as they provided fresh horses and stale beer at champagne prices. Longarm knew that, like himself, Yolanda was aware they were fencing as well as fucking. As co-conspirators for *La Causa de Mejico Libre,* their goals were much the same. But that didn't mean a receiver in stolen goods, doing business as far from Old Mexico as for God's sake *Kansas,* was anxious to see too many clients rounded up, and like Longarm, she knew who she was in bed with even as she asked to get on top.

He let her, bless her hairy but mighty bouncy chest, as he mulled over more than one fork in the trail ahead. Before hiring Alejandro Duran to murder Shadow Manners and the only member of the gang who could have said Longarm was the one he'd led as far as Wichita, Lachlan had been too well protected by his own ignorant eyes as both Longarm and the wily Billy Vail had racked their brains for any way at all to move closer.

There hadn't been one with Shadow Manners officially alive. Moving in on a face you didn't know when said face could see at a glance he'd never in this world hired you to do shit had been too big a boo. Had not Sand Lachlan ordered their deaths, Longarm and Skippy Steiner would have shook and parted friendly with Longarm holding the last of Shadow's blood money and no safe way to push it further.

He'd known when he'd gotten in Yolanda's surrey that Sand Lachlan would not be at the meeting. That was why he'd gone, stalling for time as he tried to get some forwarding addresses out of Skippy, and even if he had, the best he and Billy Vail might have managed out Cheyenne way would have been a rough-and-ready predawn sweep through no doubt a fancy hotel to arrest folks he didn't know on sight and . . . Hold on. He knew Winks Malloy on sight, thanks to pals in the tobacco trade, and he knew Malloy got rooms in fancy hotels under the name of Sullivan.

As Yolanda collapsed atop him to groan she was dying again, Longarm rolled her on her back to finish right with an elbow hooked under either knee because the last time he'd done her that way, Yolanda had gotten a wicked thrill out of being examined like a naughty little monkey in broad daylight. Fair was fair, and the same thoughts had inspired renewed interest in that position on his part. Although kissing that bearded lady in that sideshow tent that time hadn't inspired him worth mention.

Old Yolanda had her excess body hair and curvacious body parts set up just short of disgusting, and as in the case of well-aged cheese or well-hung venison, the pungent tang aroused a man's appetite for down and dirty pleasures.

Sharing a smoke after they'd died together again, Longarm "confided" that he'd likely head back to Denver unless he could figure out which way Sand and the others had gone. It didn't work. When he casually asked where *she* might suggest a customer leaving the Dexter might hole up, she said, "I do not provide such services for the people *I* deal with."

Placing a comforting hand on his flaccid organ-grinder, she explained how she and other such aiders and abettors along the Owlhoot Trail tried not to keep in touch. She said, "You know the services I provide here, and you are the first to spend a night back here with me, *querdo mio.*

I trade in . . . *bueno,* stolen goods. I just sold a popgun to a *pobrecito* who just got out of prison. When I told him was not enough gun, he said they only gave him his old clothes and half an eagle as they let him go and that everybody has to start over with something."

She began to gently stroke the matter in hand as she went on. "I took his money. I did not suggest he stay in the Dexter Hotel. I did not fix him up with a *puta* or tell him for how to get a drink in a town so dry as this one. He needed a gun. I sold him a gun. That is what I do. That is all I do."

Longarm asked if she'd sold the kid in the Texas hat any bullets for his bitty whore pistol. She said he'd said he didn't need any. When Longarm asked her if she'd ever heard of some master planner called the Dutch Uncle, she didn't answer. Her mouth was too full.

So just after sundown, served with *refritos con cerdo* with a last screwing for dessert, Longarm allowed he might see her around town sometime and hoofed it back to Douglas Avenue, where most shops were still open and a stranger in town last seen in cut-off Army gear and a straw hat could turn into somebody else.

He spent the last of the money he'd gotten for those guns down in Alamogordo, and dug into his own travel expenses to buy himself a new get-up. Longarm walked the narrow line between stylish and tinhorn in a lightweight summer suit of black Bombay silk, spun by big wild Hindu silkworms and thus not as shiny as the Chinese product gals and sissies wore.

He'd kept his boots and shoulder rig, of course, but replaced that rustic Kansas straw with a black Boss Model Stetson, its high crown creased down the front Texas-style, lest anyone confound with that lawman out Colorado way who naturally telescoped *his* more modest Stetson North Range–style.

Both hats, like his new suit, were dark for the same reasons he wore low-heeled boots without spurs. It was way harder to pussyfoot after sundown in woolly white chaps with spurs that jingled.

To appear less sneaky up close, Longarm sprang for a cheap but flashy Scotch plaid vest. The haberdasher told him it was the tartan of the Clan MacLeod. It just looked noisy to Longarm with its red and black stripes across a canary-yellow backing. He put his watch in one vest pocket and his derringer in the other, with their mutual gold-wash chain across his gut.

Then he bought a battered Gladstone in a used-baggage-and-saddle shop, weighted it some with yesterday's newspapers selling for pennies as wrapping paper, and treated himself to a sit-down shine, paying extra because his boots went up his pants so far.

He waited until shortly after a long-haul varnish had stopped at the nearby station before he moseyed into the Dexter Hotel with his back to the lace curtains of old Lenore across the way.

He wasn't sore at old Lenore. The notion of *bare* tits in the moonlight inspired fond memories indeed. But he'd told her he was a railroad dick called Henry, and that wasn't what he aimed to tell the desk clerk inside.

He set his bag down as if there'd be no discussion whether he aimed to hire a room with bath and cross-ventilation or not. The clerk told him it just so happened such a swell layout had just been vacated, but added in a worried tone, "I can't let you stay up there any later than Wednesday after next, Mister . . . ?"

"MacLeod, Doc MacLeod, they call me down home, and that would be most anywhere betwixt El Paso and San Antone, old son. Mr. Sullivan told me you'd be holding his room for him whilst he and the others are out of town on other beeswax. I told him I meant to hire it for

141

the few days I'll be here in Wichita. So do we have a deal or don't we?"

The clerk smiled and replied, "Are you sure it was Mr. Sullivan and not his associate, Mr. Bordon?"

Longarm shrugged and said, "Thought he said his name was Sullivan. We were playing cards at the time and I could have recalled the intro wrong. Big burly gent with a full black beard, going gray around the edges?"

The clerk said, "That would be our Mr. Sullivan. But I fear his room doesn't come with its own bath. Mr. *Bordon's* corner suite comes with a full bath as well as cross-ventilation. As a regular he naturally gets a rate off the management. But I fear a dollar and a half a night is the best I can do for *you*."

"At them prices you ought to throw in hot and cold running whores." Longarm sighed, adding, "Show me where to sign and let me lock this bag away so's I can see what other action Wichita has to offer a hard-up thirsty stranger."

The clerk said there was no need to register, seeing the regular who happened to be out of town was already *up* there as far as the *books* might care.

Longarm nodded knowingly and said he savvied the rules of the game. As he followed a bell boy and his bag of old newspapers up to his second-story suite, he managed not to grin like a shit-eating dog. But now he knew Sand Lachlan registered in fancy hotels as *Bordon*, and as a well traveled lawman Longarm had caught more than *that* off the smugly smiling petty crook behind the mahogany desk.

The owners of the hotel were never going to see the extra money paid for the use of any room that rented by the month, and even sneakier from the point of view of lawmen and outlaws alike, Sand Lachlan, as Bordon, would be staying in a Wichita hotel all the time he was robbing banks in Wyoming!

The bell boy let him in and handed him the room key. Longarm tipped a generous quarter instead of the usual dime, and said he'd bet another four bits the fresh-faced Kansas kid couldn't tell him where his pals, Sullivan and Bordon, might have been wetting their whistles and looking for other action around the good old Dexter in dry Kansas.

There followed the usual transient hotel hoedown, designed to keep out the hopelessly green and make life hard on the vice squad.

The bell boy asked if Mr. MacLeod was a pal of that Mr. Ross who hung out with the Misters Sullivan and Bordon.

Longarm frowned thoughtfully as if deciding. "Name's familiar. Can't put a face to it. Sullivan's the only one who'd remember me from earlier events in a certain card house. Might his pal Bordon be the shorter smooth-shaven cuss with light brown hair?"

The bell boy said he was close enough, and never mentioned Ross again. If it had been a trick question, the kid was good or somebody had put him up to it. Ross, like Lachlan and of course MacLeod, was a Scotch name.

But neither Sullivan, Steiner, Fulton, and so on back to the Carillos in the Jornado del Muerto had been Scotch, and he could be spotting sign that wasn't there.

The bell boy said he'd see what he could do as he pocketed the extra tip and turned away to see what he could do without having said or done a thing that would stand up in magistrate's court.

Longarm shut the door after him, and had a seat by the window with his hat and coat still on, knowing what came next if he hadn't been greened.

Gazing out front with his back to such lamplight as

there was in his room facing Lenore's tobacco shop and lace curtains above, Longarm didn't wave. He knew she wouldn't recognize him by tricky light at that range if she was watching for inspiration, poor lonesome thing.

He was commencing to feel lonely when there came a knock upon his hired door. So he pulled the window blind down in a natural way as he rose to his considerable height and went to see who it was.

Who it was stood about five-feet-two under piled-up taffy-colored hair in a low-cut summer frock of burnt-orange organdy. She demurely informed him that the famous spirit medium, Madame Ap Howell of Glamorgan, was planning on a midnight seance after the little social she was giving and that his friend Mr. Sullivan had suggested he might care to join them.

Longarm never blinked as your usual greenhorn might have. He knew the Sullivan who didn't really know him wouldn't be there to ask him who the hell he was. He just followed the high-toned harlot out in the hall and up two flights of stairs. Her rear view was inspiring, and along the way she delicately informed him they called her Ginger and she hadn't been reserved for later yet.

Not wanting her to take him for a mooncalf, Longarm didn't rise to that bait before he'd seen the rest of the local talent.

When Ginger led him into a larger suite than his own, as dimly lit and already blue with expensive tobacco smoke, they had one of the pimps pretending to be his old pal Sullivan until "Doc MacLeod" asked what they were trying to pull and turned as if to leave.

The pimp and the gals gathered round laughed, and told him he'd just passed his entrance exam. So he said that was more like it, and let Ginger steer him to the dry bar set up by the bodacious poker table and order him tequila without the sissy salt or lemon rind, seeing he was supposed to be just up from West Texas. A grown man could manage a neat shot of tequila without tears or a chaser if he put his mind to it, and Ginger seemed impressed.

If even one of the eight players seated around the table knew he was there, they didn't show it. There were others standing back from the main event, flirting with the gals while waiting for somebody to vacate one of exactly eight chairs. The ante started at two bits, he could see. So they were playing serious poker where a man could win or lose a working stiff's monthly salary with each hand.

He didn't spy any woman old enough to pass for a Madame Ap Anything from out of the Celtic twilight. He idly wondered if they were really to hold some sort of spooky shit later on to justify what looked more like a high-stakes poker game in the salon of a high-toned whorehouse.

Having belted back half his tequila *muy hombre,* Longarm stood there with his free arm around Ginger's trim waist to see what happened next.

What happened next was loud cussing and crashing glassware by the hall door, followed by another gal in a summer frock screaming like a scalded cat as she flew almost far as the poker table, and then, as she sat up on the rug pissing and moaning, a far taller familiar figure in a Texas hat was standing there, whore pistol in hand, to declare in a tone of no-bullshit authority, "Don't nobody move a muscle or say a word before this child tells him to. For this is a holdup and I sure hope you all understand the rules of *this* game!"

Chapter 17

A million years went by as nobody said or did a thing. Then Longarm broke the stillness by calmly declaring, "I was young and foolish once, and I can see by your hat that you hail from Texas. So I'll tell you what I'm going to do, Tex. I am going to count to ten and then, if I still see you standing there, I'm going to make you swallow that popgun without a chaser!"

The recently released con who hadn't had enough on him to buy bullets stared thunderstruck and demanded, "Wasn't you planning seeing if the sun ever rose again? I got this small but serious double-action trained to gutshoot you and . . . Where have we met before? I've seen your ugly face somewhere before."

Longarm said, "Folks point me out to you fool kids down West Texas way. They call me Doc MacLeod and as I was saying, I'll only be counting to ten. One . . . two . . . three . . ."

"Hold on, Doc! I only meant these other gents. I never meant *you*!"

Which was followed by, "Five . . . six . . . seven . . ." and on the count of eight the con wasn't there anymore.

So Longarm stepped over to help the harlot sitting on the rug to her feet as the room exploded in relieved and wondering laughter.

As Longarm turned back to the bar for another tequila, he was joined by a hatchet-faced individual in a spanking-new cheap suit of navy-blue shoddy, who soberly declared, "If our drinks weren't on the Madame, I'd buy you one, Doc. You got balls of brass or a wad of money on you. I find it easier on the nerves to leave most of my *dinero* in the hotel safe and just give a tensed-up punk my pocket jingle without making enough of a fuss to have anybody calling in the law!"

Longarm shrugged and said, "Like to have deep pockets when and if I sit down at a high-stakes poker game, and a man with a rep to worry about don't have one long after word gets around he caves in to punks."

"I've heard it ain't prudent to mess with you, Doc," replied whoever the hell he was, whether fibbing to flatter or confounded by the number of vaguely sinister young men called Doc you met up with in card houses. He added, "I got a rep too. But nobody expects you to count a man out the door when he has a gun trained on your guts at point-blank range!"

Longarm shrugged, nodded his thanks at the barkeeping brunette with a star-shaped beauty mark, and snorted, "That was no gun. It was a bitty Hargington & Richardson .32-short, and you said you had a rep too?"

The lean and hungry-looking stranger said, "Moran, they call me Frenchy Moran. I'm registered under my real name because I just got out and my release papers are in the hotel safe with most of my bankroll. I'd have let him *have* the lousy fifty and change I have on me and nobody would have called me yaller. Nobody expects us to push past tough-hairpin to damned-fool!"

Longarm said, "I suggest, as the easygoing sport I am,

147

you never again call me a damned fool unless you really mean it. I think I've heard tell of you, Frenchy. The late Skippy Steiner made mention of an Irishman they called Frenchy because he fucked with his mouth and fought with his feet."

Frenchy blinked and said, "Skippy was killed right here in Wichita and just the other night! You knew him, Doc?"

Longarm threw back the shot of tequila and managed not to wheeze as he replied, "Not here in Wichita. I just got in this evening. But of course I read about him and what's his name—Shadow Martin?—shooting it out with a famous greaser the other night."

Frenchy said, "Manners. Shadow Manners. Where did you know Skippy from if it wasn't here in Wichita?"

Longarm replied without pause, "Alamogordo. Skippy, Shadow Manners, and me spent some time there at Texas Red's. They left before I did. I had a chore to tend in Waco before I headed up this way to . . . I am still talking to a pal of Old Skippy, ain't I?"

Frenchy said, "You are, and when the three of you were down New Mexico way, did Skippy make mention of a gal named Hazel?"

Longarm, as Doc MacLeod, replied in a dismissive tone, "Not to me. He did say to look him up here in Kansas at that perfumed bathhouse he stayed at. Said he might be able to put me on to something bigger than my . . . chore in Waco."

He saw something big turning away in the depths of Frenchy's sea-green eyes and tossed in, "Funny you should ask about them having a gal riding with 'em, though. I didn't 'tend the inquest. That many lawmen under one roof upsets my stomach. But there *was* all this talk about the two of them, Skippy and that other cuss, riding in with three mounts, one of 'em sidesaddled. I can't say how Skippy 'splained that. Like I said, I wasn't there."

"I read the transcripts," Frenchy cut in, explaining. "Skippy bragged some on how him and Shadow saved some old greaser gal under assumed names down Alamogordo way. I only got to talk to him once, and old Sand cut in before I could get it clear in my head about my Hazel. You know Sand, of course?"

Longarm shook his head and said, "Never met your Hazel in Alamogordo neither. Only mutual pal Skippy mentioned to this child was Winks Malloy, or Mr. Sullivan as they have him registered here."

As Longarm kept a gentle thumb on the reel, Frenchy Moran insisted, "Are you dead certain neither Skippy nor Shadow ever mentioned that sidesaddle they rode off in the desert with while the three of you were at Texas Red's?"

Reeling out more line, Longarm started to say he hadn't, frowned in thought, and then confided, "They might have told old Texas Red. I remember her saying something about somebody likely to be mighty sore about that empty saddle. Can't say who she meant, though."

Frenchy soberly replied, "You don't have to. But now the ones who could have told me what in blue blazes poor little Hazel was doing out in the damned desert to begin with can never begin to tell me, and Texas Red was right. I'm sore as hell!"

"You mean your leader, Lakeshore or whatever, couldn't tell you what she was doing out yonder for him?" asked Longarm innocently.

Frenchy said, "Sand didn't know. Said he'd worked things out with others to help Skippy get Shadow out of the desert once he had to hop off that train. Sand thought that hired gun Shadow might have asked her to tag along. That's how come, when he first heard Shadow was here

149

in Wichita, looking for Skippy, he told Skippy to bring him here for a set-down and protracted conversation about details Skippy might have missed."

Frenchy signaled the pretty barkeep as he added with a frustrated sigh, "Lord only knows why the two of them wound up in that hog farm shoot-out instead. Sand says Shadow Manners must have known Alejandro Duran from down along the border. The greaser wasn't riding for anybody *Sand* knew all that well!"

As Frenchy consumed his bourbon and branch water, another innocent-looking and hence high-priced whore came over to sweetly but firmly inform them there would be no seance that night and the party was over.

Neither well-traveled gent at the bar asked how come.

Longarm's eyes met those of the one called Ginger, staring at him through the already thinning tobacco smoke. When he pointed at her, himself, and the hall door, Ginger nodded and drifted their way to join them just as Frenchy was asking where they might continue their conversation.

Then he smiled thinly and said, "Never mind, Doc. I know which room you're staying in, and don't leave before you check back with me. I may have something you might be interested in later in the week."

Longarm allowed he was game for any action that didn't draw blood, and left with Ginger to prove it. He knew they knew their pal the room clerk was pocketing the extra hire of Lachlan's quarters, and had no call to ask what some of 'em were grinning about.

Longarm had long since vowed that if money wouldn't buy love, it was just plain stupid to pay for hostility. So paying gals like Ginger was against his code when he had anything to say about it. But he knew a tinhorn such as the one he was playing would prefer a financial transaction in a strange town to his own manly fist, and put the money atop the dresser by her door without comment lest she take him for a stranger to her world.

As she shucked her duds with the practiced ease of a professional banana peeler, Longarm was able to recall more distasteful chores he'd performed in the cause of justice. For she was built like those gals on the higher-priced French postcards and ginger-haired all over.

Tossing her summer frock over the back of a chair, the sass pranced to the window overlooking the street to raise the shades with a dirty laugh.

Longarm trimmed the bedside lamp, protesting, "If I aimed to put on a burlesque show for downtown Wichita, I'd sell tickets, girl!"

Ginger giggled and said, "Hardly anybody can see all the way in far as the bed, save from one window across the way. There's this old maid who rooms above a tobacco shop and she thinks we don't know what she's up to. She thinks she's so smart. She never moves her lace curtain when her lamp is trimmed. But when it's lit, you can see her in her unmentionables! My chum Kitty thinks she plays with herself over yonder as she peeks across through her curtains. Sometimes we put on shows for the dirty-minded old baggage!"

Longarm snorted, "Takes one to know one, I reckon. But old maids are the least of my worries when you consider a Springfield .45-70 can kill at a mile and them rooftops across the way are more like twenty-five yards."

So she pulled the blind back down and they got to watch themselves in two mirrors by lamplight as Ginger put on a show indeed, on top. He was sincerely glad Lenore, across the way, couldn't see what they were up to, even as picturing Lenore in the same position in contrast with old hairy Yolanda inspired his old organ-grinder to greater heights.

By the time he managed to come in Ginger, he'd had

to evoke memories all the way back to West-by-God Virginia in a hayloft. For it confounded a man's feelings to have it in the sweetest-looking little thing since leaving Denver when he just plain didn't *like* her.

So before noon the next morning it was established up and down the back stairs of the Dexter Hotel that the famous Doc MacLeod from West Texas took no shit off male or female and had somebody gunning for him with a Springfield sniper's rifle, likely with a telescopic sight.

But you couldn't tell until along about sundown, as he was supping in the Dexter dining room. Frenchy Moran joined him, asking his permission first before sitting down, and said, "They left me here to wait for some other West Texas riders. My pals who've gone on to Wyoming just wired that the five of those riders have been given more than enough time to get here. So we're short five guns. Are you interested?"

Longarm sliced his steak thoughtfully and replied, "Not with all them loose cannons on the deck. Who might we be talking about? I know most of the real hairpins out of West Texas."

Frenchy easily replied, "They were told to look me up once they got up here because I'm using my real name till the heat dies down. Sand said I would know them when they mentioned the Eagle Saloon in El Paso, see?"

Longarm saw indeed. He tried to picture himself being that stupid, and decided Billy Vail might get away with lying to him that boldly. It didn't take a college degree to lie to those who trusted you.

Once he'd put away the morsel of meat, Longarm muttered, "Five of 'em? Never showed up before Lachlan left town, after he'd sent all the way to Texas for the five of 'em? I dunno, Frenchy, what if they've been picked up, knowing what they know about . . . Wyoming?"

Frenchy said, "They don't. All they were told by night

152

letter was that our bunch and some others would be taking part in a joint venture of the Dutch Uncle. You've heard tell of him, of course?"

Longarm sipped some coffee thoughtfully and grudgingly conceded, "I reckon every good old boy up this way must have. Albeit all I know is that he's supposed to be one hell of an engineer. But if you know what his plans for Wyoming would be . . ."

Frenchy said, "I don't. The Dutch Uncle offers only them instructions needed, just before they're to be carried out. If the fucking feds were to pick me up this evening and stake me out on an ant pile, I wouldn't be able to tell them more than I'm telling you, Doc."

"What *are* you telling me?" asked Longarm.

Frenchy said, "All I know for certain is that it's big. The Dutch Uncle don't set up penny-ante games. I was told to lag behind here to wait for them Texans and see if anybody sniffed around this hotel after they sort of drifted off without notice. This afternoon I wired Sand at the Cheyenne address he left me, telling him them other Texans hadn't shown and 'scribing you as worth five average Texans. So later this evening Sand wired I was to join him and the boys in Wyoming and bring you along if I had you down as a serious sporting man. So how's about it, Doc? Are you in?"

"In *what*?" laughed Longarm in his Texas badman style. "You remind me of this sweet señorita I met at this dance they were holding for some saint. When she asked if I wanted to come along with her, she failed to mention her surly kinfolk in that dark alley and, no offense, Frenchy, you ain't half as tempting as she was!"

"I can promise you'll come out ahead by four figures, with no chance of getting caught."

The man he was trying to recruit said, "There's always

a chance of getting caught. Didn't you say you just got out of prison?"

Frenchy said, "That's where I first heard about the Dutch Uncle. I was smart enough starting out. I was never caught in the act riding for anybody. Somebody peached me to the law in Dodge, just as we were fixing to relocate here to Wichita. I copped a plea to three at hard, and got out early as agreed. But the time spent fucking my fist and wishing it was Hazel resolved me never to be taken alive again."

He looked away and said, "You'd know what I was talking to if you'd ever laid eyes on my Hazel, Doc. Words cannot describe how pretty she was, even with her duds on, and once she had 'em off . . ."

"I get the picture," Longarm cut in, truthfully enough. "I'll study on it. Throwing in with you and the Dutch Uncle, not your Hazel. I like to see the board set up before I make my first move. Playing checkers in the dark with folk I don't know just ain't my style."

Frenchy said, "You got till ten tonight at the latest. There's a ten-twenty night train leaving for Omaha and the cross-country line to Cheyenne, and I aim to be aboard her, with or without you, Doc."

Chapter 18

The railroads liked to shuffle their passenger combinations about after dark for the same reasons Western Union gave night-letter rates when business conducted by wire was slow. The real money in railroading was hauling freight. They'd have let the public be damned if state and federal regulators hadn't insisted they provide some service to voting taxpayers in exchange for all those rights of passage across public land as well as government grants. So, seeing they had to provide passenger service, they shoehorned it in where it didn't get too much in the way of coal or corn or cows that didn't have to be coddled or, hell, even offered a seat.

So Frenchy Moran and his pal "Doc" got into Omaha at that christawful hour when the cows have been milked and the roosters are waiting for the sun to come up and hear them crow.

They had to lay over in Omaha for a late-afternoon westbound varnish. Knockabout gents who were strangers in town stayed off the streets of the town until they were ready to move on. Frenchy had already told him along the way they'd be holing up for the day in a quality hotel where gents were expected to wear ties in the dining room and not bring in any whores of color. But he asked how come when Frenchy led them south along the platform while all the others getting off seemed to be headed north to the depot.

Frenchy said, "Omaha P.D. initiates new plainclothes by letting them rise and shine early and greet incoming trains with fists full of wanted posters."

Longarm truthfully replied, "I don't have my current handle on any fucking wanted poster, and you say you're packing release papers!"

Frenchy said, "Either way, be it recorded, Officer honey, neither of them handsome faces ever smiled at Omaha P.D. because they ain't *watching* platforms that ain't in use nor in easy view of the ones they are watching."

So saying, he tossed his overnight bag ahead of him into the dark and followed it off the far end of the long plank platform.

Longarm hung on to his secondhand Gladstone as he estimated about where the ground might be and jumped. He landed a tad off balance, but wouldn't have fallen even if Frenchy hadn't grabbed an arm to steady him.

As he thanked his fellow traveler, he made a mental note that Frenchy was even stronger than he looked. You could hide a lot of whipcord and whale-bone inside a long, lean suit of shoddy.

Glancing back the way they'd come, he saw how they had a clear view of anything or anybody outlined against the station lamps while, at the same time, they were invisible to anybody out on any of the platforms.

As he followed his guide along that stretch of the Owl-hoot Trail, the graceful cuss who managed to look stylish in prison-tailored shoddy, he marveled as ever at the convoluted criminal mind. For he'd long since come to the conclusion that, like less menacing poets, inventors, or novelists, born crooks just couldn't lay out a trip to the corner for a bucket of beer as the simple chore it was when they could turn it into a sly game of chess, and then cheat at the game.

But try telling your average whore she could make as much or more as waitress in a given year when you factored all the time she spent doing nothing with a lamppost as she froze her ass, and she'd sweetly tell you her pimp had her down as his best earner. For folks who chose to live by their so-called wits didn't count the wasted hours of their lives as a part of the sporting life.

He'd gotten to sort of like old Frenchy in the time they'd palled along the Owlhoot Trail. But he knew he'd never make him see that when you put an unpaid year in prison on the scales with a trail hand's dollar or so a day, the trail hand came out way ahead on his rambling or gambling alone. But Doc MacLeod out of West Texas wouldn't have thought so either. So he and Longarm held their peace as they followed Frenchy across the yards in the dark.

Then they didn't seem alone in the dark beyond the view from the depot. Longarm muttered, "Know any other swell shortcuts, pard?" as a wolfpack of hobos or worse materialized across their path.

A bigger one with a baseball bat demanded in a jovial tone, "And what might we be having in them bags that we didn't want the copper badges to be asking about, Slim?"

Then things happened too fast for Longarm to keep track as he threw the Gladstone full of newspapers at one near him while he went for his shoulder-holstered .44-40.

But when he got it out, there was nobody handy to aim it at. One writhed at Frenchy's feet, grasping his shattered knee in the silent agony of a trapped wolf, while the one Frenchy had kicked in the head just lay there.

The others were already out of sight, running low to present less tempting targets as they studied on the error of their ways.

Frenchy said, "Fuck the baggage. Follow me!" So Longarm ran after him as somewhere in the night a police whistle trilled.

He'd thought those hobos had acted bold back there. Offering to serve as a police informer could cut a petty thug a lot of slack.

The two travelers the hobos never should have messed with ducked under a platform to work their way along the strip of darkness under it like a pair of crabbing bats until they were under the depot itself, seated on dry dirt with their backs to a shared brick pilaster.

Frenchy said, "Fuck! I tore the knee out of this cheap prison shoddy!"

Longarm didn't find that surprising. Shoddy, or reclaimed wool, was made by shredding old clothes in a sort of cotton gin until you wound up with separated but short-staple fibers you could spin and weave into a product that looked like virgin wool, felt like virgin wool, but didn't stand up to wear much better than paper.

Longarm suggested, "Raggedy duds and no baggage don't cut much ice if you offer to pay in advance where the lobby lamps ain't bright."

Frenchy said, "We ain't supposed to stay no place but the Dunbarton Arms on Harney Steet. We get a rate there, and the Dutch Uncle advises us to go there and stay there, sending out for anything we want till we're ready to move on out of town."

Longarm didn't answer. He was thinking back to the last case he'd worked there in Omaha. The parts he knew best were mostly fairgrounds and stockyards, but he knew his way around Butchertown, the complex of slaughter-houses, tanneries, tallow-rendering plants, and so forth, along with the saloons, cheap boardinghouses, and shabbier hotels catering to a turnover trade of trail drivers, cattle buyers, and such.

He said, "No offense, Frenchy, but we'd best let me take the lead here in Omaha. I know the town. Your Dutch Uncle is right about the law keeping an eye on the the dance halls and whorehouses, but I know this small hotel up a side street where trail bosses and such rest up a night or more before heading home. So here's what we ought to do."

"We're supposed to dammit follow orders!" Frenchy declared.

Longarm said soothingly, "I ain't under orders from nobody yet. Like I told you back in Wichita, I ain't saying I'm in or out before I meet this wizard of criminal enterprise and see what he has in mind this time. So, like I was saying, we'll get you in that torn prison outfit off the street to start with. Then I'll toss that suit over my arm and carry it far as a shop I know in Butchertown where paid-off trail drivers like to gussy up like men of destiny for their train rides home."

Hearing no argument, he went on, "I'll pick us up more baggage lest the Union Pacific porters this evening make note of mysterious well-dressed gents traveling without baggage and, worse yet, having no good excuse to tip the going and forgettable rate."

Frenchy finally agreed. Frenchy was just too trusting to ride the Owlhoot Trail with the likes of Sand Lachlan. He wasn't *totally* stupid.

They worked their way along a brick foundation wall to an open trap used by maintanance workers, and nobody said anything when the two of them strode out of the door marked EMPLOYEES ONLY.

Outside, they found it was almost broad day, and Frenchy was cussing his torn pants every step of the way till Longarm called a halt at a newsstand and bought him a newspaper, saying, "Hold this rolled up at one end and loose at the other. Brush it back and forth across your knee as we walk. It ain't too far, and nobody's going to remember that suit in any case."

Frenchy protested, after catching sight of himself in a shop window, that the paper wasn't hiding his exposed kneecap all that well. But when Longarm suggested he toss the paper aside, Frenchy hung on to it.

Butchertown was handy to the far side of the railroad yards, and Frenchy felt a lot better in his underwear and Schofield .45 upstairs as his pal "Doc" went shopping for him.

Once he was free of Frenchy, Longarm's first stop was a tad out of the way at a Western Union, where he wired an urgent plea for travel expenses. For he was about tapped out and Doc MacLeod was said to be a high roller.

Then, knowing it would take at least an hour or more for Denver to say yes or no, he found a tailor catering to the cattle industry.

The friendly but world-weary older man behind the counter fingered the torn shoddy pants and said, "So, somebody just got out of prison and went up a flight of stairs too fast? Confidential, this *schlock* is not worth patching. Any cloth I patched it with would outlast such a suit!"

Longarm said, "I know. My pal who just got out needs real duds to look for a job in. I was hoping you might have something never reclaimed after a cleaning, in the same size?"

The tailor held the jacket up to the light, thought, and decided, "The width at waist and shoulders I got. The sleeves of the jacket and cuffs of the pants need taking in. Have you got five dollars including alterations and a couple of hours I could use off and on in the back?"

Longarm said he surely did as he smiled sincerely. For the timing worked out swell. He paid two up front and left empty-handed, but picked up a half-dozen sandwiches and some bottled beer to carry back to the hotel.

As he rejoined Moran, seated on the bed in his underwear with the morning paper across his knees, Frenchy declared, "There's something fishy as all hell going on. For according to what I just read, somebody has been *lying* to this child and he don't like it much!"

Longarm calmly asked what they were talking about as he unpacked his brown bags on the dresser top.

Frenchy said, "Some D&RG trackwalkers just found Shadow Manners in a railroad culvert. What was left of him leastways. He'd been chawed some by the floodwaters that had scraped and bumped him that far across the Jornado del Muerto, and what with the heat and bugs and bigger desert critters, it took them forty-eight hours to figure who the fuck he was. But that's who he was. Had this well-known tattoo as well as gold front teeth."

Longarm truthfully replied, "I don't recall meeting up with any gold front teeth down Alamogordo way."

As he opened a couple of beers with his jackknife, Frenchy demanded, "Then who in the hell was staying at Texas Red's as Shadow Manners if the real Shadow Manners lay moldering in a railroad culvert on the far side of the San Andres Mountains?"

Longarm handed over a ham on rye with Frenchy's beer as he replied in a disinterested tone, "Somebody else who was just saying he was a well-known killer, I reckon. I was in no position to argue, seeing I'd never met up with the real Shadow Manners. Your pal Skippy sure kept *calling* the jasper Shadow. He must have thought that was who he was talking to. But what the hell, the both of

161

them lay dead in the Wichita morgue along with them other unclaimed bodies. I got you a swell nearly new suit. Coffee-brown. Going back for it this afternoon. Needed taking in."

Frenchy washed some ham and cheese on rye with his beer, but kept on chewing with his mind. He asked Longarm to repeat earlier descriptions of the man they'd taken for the man Sand Lachlan had sent to gun Clem Aherne. Once Longarm had, Frenchy mused, "Tall, good-looking, smooth-shaven . . . Any fool can shave smooth if he puts his mind to it. I think I got it."

Longarm set his hat aside and forked himself over a bentwood chair to stuff his own face with an expression of desperate disinterest.

Frenchy said, "Add her up. Exactly two men jumped off the night train in the middle of that desert. One was Shadow, who'd just gunned Clem, and the other was the famous lawman, Longarm!"

The famous Longarm mildy demurred, "Papers say he's in a Denver hospital right now, pard."

The animated Frenchy insisted, "Bullshit! That was all a cover-up! I see it all now. Longarm and the real Shadow shot it out in the desert and Longarm won. Then he stumbled on the escape route Sand had set up, and as soon as Skippy Steiner mistook him for Shadow, the sneaky lawman saw the chance to be led by the hand straight to the rest of us! I've read in other papers how Longarm could be sneaky like that. So, right, Longarm fooled Skippy, Texas Red, yourself, and all the others until he and Skippy met up with that famous Mexican gun, who likely *knew* the real Shadow from down along the border and . . . You're right! We don't have to worry about *any* of them old boys no more!"

So both of them cheered up and that afternoon, when Longarm said he'd go see if that suit was ready, Frenchy asked him to drop by Western Union along the way and wire Sand and the boys for him.

Longarm was more than willing. Once he'd picked up and cashed a money order there, he wired a rambling night letter for Uncle Billy to decode.

Frenchy cottoned to his new suit, and old "Doc" was too good a sport to tell Frenchy what the duds had cost, let alone take money from a pal.

Frenchy made up for it by booking them Pullman berths aboard the night train to Cheyenne. So they got in rested, but still wound up with swell hotel rooms when Frenchy did all the talking at the desk.

He'd been expected, so they had a sealed envelope for him. On the way up Frenchy opened it, and told Longarm they were expected at a gathering of the clans on the top floor that afternoon.

So they parted friendly, and each managed a few more hours of rest, with a shower and a shave thrown in, before they met in the hall and went on up to the connected top-floor suites the Dutch Uncle had set up for a swell brawl.

As Longarm and Frenchy went in, things were already getting started. A whore pretty enough to be an actress took their hats. The buffet was already being served along one wall, and yonder, by the exit to a terrace, a piano was tinkling one of those afternoon-tea tunes that didn't call for much attention as a rule.

But as he tried to decide whether the piano was tinkling "Aura Lee" or "Rally Round the Flag, Boys," Longarm saw who they'd hired to play that infernal upright, and suddenly felt as if he was out on that terrace and about to be pushed over the rail!

Chapter 19

They called her Red Robin because she said her name was Robin, and her hair and low-cut velveteen gown were as red as she could afford. The shapely little thing didn't put out if she didn't like you, and she played piano like a tone-deaf kitten on the keys. But she'd shot a man in Chicago, and hence tended to be welcome at such gatherings.

Longarm was one of many Red Robin liked, a lot, and she tended to let it show because planting a big wet kiss on one of the taller men in the joint was a good way to keep some of the others from trying to cop a feel as a girl was trying to play the fucking piano.

So before she could get them in trouble, Longarm picked up a paper napkin, broke out a stub pencil, and wrote, "Might you play 'Memories of a Night in Paso Robles'?" signed it Doc MacLeod, and bet a waiter a nickel he wouldn't run it over to her.

So when she twisted in her seat to look him over, cool as a butcher's cat, he knew she remembered that other time he'd been working in secret and she'd almost gotten him killed by calling him by name.

Someone else was calling him Doc, and he turned to see Frenchy and a snotty smiler who answered to the descriptions he had of Sand Lachlan even though, as ever, the real face didn't go with the one he'd imagined.

As they shook, Lachlan glanced down at the noisy tartan vest to laugh and say, "Well, of *course* this would be Doc MacLeod. Can you imagine any white man wearing that nigger-yellow plaid if he had any other clan to call his own?"

He told Longarm, "Glad to have you aboard, Doc. Frenchy here says he's seen you crawfish a man who had the drop on you and that the two of you go back a ways."

Longarm wasn't about to argue. When Frenchy said Doc had known poor old Skippy too, Longarm said, "Just to talk to. Never rid with Skippy. Met him at Texas Red's in Alamogordo, and he said to look him up if ever I got to Wichita. But by the time I got there he'd gone down in a shoot-out."

Frenchy said, "We was just talking about that. Tell him, Sand."

Lachlan looked like he wanted to hug himself for being so smart as he confided, "Only took one wire to another member of The Web in Denver to find out the feds were fucking with us. Nobody who looked anything like Longarm's been in Denver General all this time. Only way it adds up is the way Frenchy puts it together. As I was just now explaining, Alejandro Duran and them other Texicans were the extra help I'd been expecting to join us in Wichita. Knowing Alejandro and the real Shadow Manners worked together in the past, I suggested Skippy gather everybody in one place and make sure the coast was clear before he brung 'em to the Dexter."

Longarm whistled and said, "Good thing you did! Imagine what might have happened at the Dexter had Skippy showed up with ignorant Texicans and a famous lawman to plot a . . . What are we plotting here, Sand?"

Lachlan said, "Ain't certain. The Dutch Uncle must have something big in mind. He's called the Bitter Creek Boys and the Dugans of Durango as well to this meeting. Over fifty guns as I add her up. But you know how he likes to hold his cards to his vest."

Longarm knew no such thing, but he nodded and grabbed a wine flute off a passing tray. To his mild surprise, it was real champagne. Whoever in hell the Dutch Uncle was, he wasn't slow.

A lean mean-looking cuss joined them to be introduced as Lash Dugan of Durango. Not wanting to be taken for a greenhorn, Dugan naturally said he'd heard good things about Doc MacLeod out of West Texas. But then they were joined by the burly bearded Winks Malloy, also known as Sullivan, and while Longarm recognized Winks on sight, Winks had never laid eyes on Longarm before. So he looked a tad confounded when Longarm stuck out a hand and said, "Howdy, Winks," before anyone could introduce them.

Winks asked uncertainly, "Do I know you?"

Longarm laughed and said, "Not sober. The Long Branch, in Dodge, the night they threw that cowboy out for slapping leather?"

Then Red Robin joined them to declare a break and ask if they had any requests as she slipped a bare arm through Longarm's to lightly add, "Nice to see you again, Doc."

Sand asked, "You know old Doc, Miss Robin?"

She smile dirty and replied, "Let's just say we go back to a gold rush out California way. Sometimes things pan out and sometimes they don't."

So Winks Malloy decided, "Well, *sure* I recall that night in the Long Branch now that I think back. You were right, Doc. I was drunk. I was always drunk in Dodge, before I learned to act high-toned in public."

So Red Robin asked Longarm to smear some of that "patted frog grass" on a cracker and walk her back over to the piano. That gave him a chance to murmur, "Ain't got time for a song and dance. Let's just say I seem to have throwed in with something big. Might you have the least notion what they have in mind, Miss Robin?"

She set the saucer of hors d'oeuvres along with a hotel tumbler of champagne she'd managed herself atop the piano, and stayed on her feet as she murmured with a sweetly blank expression, "Big is the word you were groping for. I just work here. They hired me away from a less ritzy-titzy hotel for this shindig. You want me to pump the other help for what I can find out about our gracious host, Custis?"

He said, "I surely would. I'm staying in Room 3-E. If you see a match stem on the floor outside my door, it'll be safe to knock. If it ain't there you better not. Will you be off by midnight?"

She said, "Sooner. I was told this shindig means to break up by sundown. Shall we say orgy at eight?"

He laughed and said, "Better make it after nine. I may have way less pleasant chores to tend to."

She sat down, purring, "Is that what you call doing me dog-style, a *chore,* you brute?" Then she proceeded to play "Coming Through the Rye," unless it was "The Gerry Owen." It got even tougher to tell when Red Robin was trying to play high-toned and soft.

Whatever she was doing at the piano, somebody else was tinging a fork on the stem of a wine flute for attention. So Longarm turned round to pay attention. It came easy when you felt tense.

The white-haired figure of authority in a suit that cost more than a year's salary tinged the fork again and said, "I see all the leaders of our various . . . factions are here, and I have a train to catch. So what if I issue my written instructions to each leader and review some of our usual but very important withdrawal tactics?"

Nobody argued, so the Dutch Uncle, as he figured to be, continued. "I know some of you younger riders feel I'm an old fuss. But I can't stress too hard that while anybody can hold up a stage, a train, or a bank, you have to know what you're doing to *get away with it*!"

He waited for the murmur of approval to die before he went on. "Nobody with a lick of common sense gets in trouble going *into* a bank, and if he and his backup know their oats, it's not hard to cope with the customers and staff and grab the money and *start* your run. So that's where things start to break down."

Longarm wasn't the only one there who muttered, "That's for sure."

The Dutch Uncle said, "We've all had time to go over the Northfield Raid of the James-Younger gang. We all know they were among the best of the old-time guerrilla raiders, and we all know how things went to hell in a hack as they were *trying to get away*!"

Winks Malloy said, "I heard some townsmen recognized 'em and spread the word."

The Dutch Uncle nodded and asked, "Let's consider why that happened. When you look at it carefully none of those Northfield farmers recognized a particular gang member. They recognized a *gang*. Frank's or Jesse's idea of wearing slickers to the robbery so they could cast them aside and ride on in different costumes would have worked, had they all worn different brands of rain slickers, travel dusters, and what all. It was the sight of all those identical slickers on strangers riding in that alerted the townsmen, with the result that only Frank and Jesse got away in the end."

He tinged his fork to hush the buzz and went on. "They

168

were luckier than they deserved that day. Had all of them ridden out unscathed, they had no sensible *getaway* planned. They just rode, like foxes in front of the hounds, with local posses chasing them through country they didn't know with no place to hole up! They behaved, in short, like kids raiding an apple orchard."

Sand Lachlan laughed and said, "So tell us what we're fixing to raid instead and how we're going to get away so slick."

The Dutch Uncle said, "The target is the Cheyenne branch of Uncle Pete, the Union Pacific Railroad. The prize is over a million squirreled away to pay out as bills and wages at the end of this fiscal quarter. The team assigned to go in and open the vaults will have the combination. Others will be drawing the law across town with the riot we've arranged, topped off with arson and black powder. As I said, each of you will have his own instructions to follow, and needn't concern himself with what others may or may not do until we're all safely back in Wichita dividing up the take."

Not everyone there cheered. Sand Lachlan said, "I've yet to cash some of them securites you told us we could consider good as gold."

The Dutch Uncle shrugged and said, "They *are* good as gold, in Mexico. I advised you to cash them there. What happened? Where are they now?"

"Bank vault in El Paso, I hope," said Sand, adding, "You forgot to tell them Bronco Apache I wanted to bank in Mexico."

The Dutch Uncle looked pained and said, "This next haul will be cash. Mostly specie. As you study your instructions tonight, you'll see how I laid out different diversions to help you all fade into the confusion and make your way back to this rather fancy hotel where one would

•

hardly expect to brush elbows with wild and woolly sorts."

That drew applause as well as laughter. The Dutch Uncle said, "Very well. Enjoy the refreshments and entertainments up here in the sky where only your friends can peek. Then all of you should try for a good night's sleep off the streets in a respectable hotel and . . . Hell, boys, you know the way we've been hiding you where nobody's looking for you!"

Then he left. More than one gunslick assembled sneered at the way the older man covered his expensively costumed ass by leaving town before a pin dropped. But Sand Lachlan pointed out, and Lash Dugan agreed, that nobody had expected General Robert E. Lee to lead Pickett's Charge. For if rank had no privilages, who'd want the fucking rank?

The party got rowdier after the man throwing it had left. But as the Dutch Uncle had suggested, who else in Cheyenne knew shit?

So nobody noticed as Longarm slipped out for a spell, and got back just in time to haul an amorous drunk off Red Robin. The drunk was a good sport about it when Doc MacLeod explained they were working on an opera together.

So a discreet two hours later, they were making sweet music down in Longarm's digs, and as ever Red Robin reminded him of a curvacious ivory base fiddle as he played her dog-style, the most conversational position for long-established lovers.

Arching her spine to take it deeper, Red Robin said, "The girls say the Dutch Uncle is a defrocked priest, a disbarred lawyer, or this real-estate speculator who did ten at hard in Leavenworth and got out back in '74, during that railroad scandal and business bust, to buy himself a hotel cheap somewhere in Kansas."

Gently but firmly clasping a hipbone in either hand as he moved in and out at a teasing tempo, Longarm mused, "Educated high-toned gents meet way more owlhoot riders in prison than at their country clubs. He must have been shocked by their crude manners, whilst they found his helpful hints as eye-opening."

She purred, "Do me faster, and how come anyone with a lick of common sense would have to be told you're only looking to be stopped by the law when you wear tattoos and dress up like a Gypsy pimp?"

Thrusting faster, Longarm explained, "Folks with a lick of common sense seldom choose to ride the Owlhoot Trail. Makes our job easier when those who do advertise their calling in the dance halls honest men don't drink in. You'd think they'd wise up to the way they give themselves away. But seems they're willing to cut this Dutch Uncle in for a share if only he'll tell them how to use common sense."

Picking up the tempo was having the same effect on Longarm. So he rolled Red Robin on her shapely rear to finish right, stiff-armed and long-donging her deep as she bitched he was killing her and she'd kill him if he stopped before she came.

So he didn't, and as they shared a smoke atop the rumpled bedding, she sighed and said, "Thanks, I needed that. I keep forgetting how swell we fit together down yonder until I see you again and it all comes back to make me warm and wet. I wish there was a way to have it like that every night without being stuck with one man."

He snuggled her closer and said, "Me too, but as we have already agreed on other such occasions, the two of us would likely wind up fighting over whose turn it was to wash or wipe if we ever lived together long enough for the surprise to wear off. We'd better try for a few hours sleep, honey. I set the alarm clock I just picked up for four A.M. and we want to be up and dressed, with me sporting my badge and you sworn in as my deputy, when the others show up."

Red Robin asked, "Is that what I hear ticking? What are you talking about, Custis? The big robbery the Dutch Uncle and the three gangs staying here had planned was for later in the morning, wasn't it?"

Longarm said, "It had to be. Uncle Pete's Cheyenne business offices won't be open any earlier. But if we wait for fifty-odd outlaws in three gangs to make their first moves and try to shoot them on the rise, innocent folk could get hurt and some of them would be sure to get away."

He snuffed out the cheroot and added, "The federal, state, and county law I spoke with earlier this evening agreed there was nothing in the Good Book or the U.S. Constitution that said you couldn't nip a crime in the bud. And before you ask about rules of evidence, we don't *need* evidence all the crooks lying slugabed under this very roof meant to hit anywhere here in Cheyenne this morning. Every blamed one of them is wanted for a lot of other robberies in a heap of other parts."

So they caught forty winks, woke up to screw again, and that was the way things were going by the time they were dressed and standing in the doorway, looking stern in the name of the law as all hell kept busting loose around them.

The Bitter Creek Boys gave up without a fight. Lash Dugan died with one boot on and one boot off as the state troopers who'd kicked in his door gave him his choice and he chose to go down fighting.

Winks Malloy, also known as Sullivan, went down the stairs ass-over-teakettle, but didn't feel the bumps and scrapes with those two hundred grains of hot lead in his brain.

So as the smoke was clearing, the score stood fourteen dead and thirty-six wanted outlaws captured with only two local lawmen flesh-wounded. But even as they were congratulating one another all around, the Dutch Uncle had left town hours earlier and somehow, amid all the confusion, both Sand Lachlan and Frenchy Moran had gotten away clean.

Chapter 20

For all his educated high-toned ways, the self-styled master criminal whose real name was Ajax J. Wilberforce, was the one they caught first. Having lectured his uncouth outlaw associates on the smart ways to pussyfoot past the law with proper-duds and manners in the proper parts of town, the Dutch Uncle didn't know beans about just plain running for it, and there were times it was smarter to pussyfoot and there were times it was smarter to just plain *run*!

So by the time Longarm was reunited with his recovered Stetson and dry-cleaned tweed suit of a Saturday and reported to Billy Vail the next Monday, the older, shorter, and dumpier Vail was feeling mighty pleased with his own long-distance arrest, having tracked their Dutch Uncle through dry and dusty paper files as slick as a bloodhound sniffing through woods and swamplands after a fugitive's genuine stink.

Actually inviting Longarm to sit down and light up, with a rare smile on his usually grumpy visage, Billy Vail said, "You were right about that hotel in Cheyenne being owned and managed by the same landlord. He owned rental properties in and around Wichita and hither and yon all over these parts."

As Longarm lit a cheroot in self-defense, Billy Vail puffed far more pungent smoke his way and bragged, "Henry and me, with the help of Western Union, were able to track old Ajax from both directions until both paper trails crossed at his fancy home address in Topeka. For like you wired us, there could only be a finite number of well-educated high-toned crooks released from Leavenworth in the Year of Our Lord 1874. From there his paper trail led to that first transient hotel he bought, cheap, during the financial depression of the early seventies. Once we determined he'd not only showed a profit, but plowed the profit back into more property during a buyer's market, it was easy to see he'd started to sell respectable cover to disreputable drifters the local law would have expected to find in the usual haunts on the seedier side of Main Street."

Longarm nodded soberly and remarked, "Once he'd gone into the business of offering shelter for the night along the Owlhoot Trail, it was only a step further to hold classes on the finer points of evading the law, and from there it followed as the night the day the Dutch Uncle would know a lot more than your average illiterate about choosing targets."

Vail said, "That's for certain. Left to their own devices, honest young cowboys gone wrong tend to hold up poor people or steal shit they can't sell for drinking money. Had all his pupils been honest young cowboys gone wrong, the Dutch Uncle's setup might have lasted way longer. But thanks to you and the wild-ass ways of the murderous Sand Lachlan, the Dutch Uncle is fixing to be a distinguished old man indeed by the next time he aids, abets, and lectures crooks as an expert on the subject."

"Likely drooling some," Longarm agreed, noting, "He's

sure to spend the next twenty years pondering the error of his ways, and he's got to be well on the way to seventy as we speak."

Vail said, "Already seventy-two. I asked. So let's not worry about him as we consider the two more dangerous ones still at large."

Taking another drag on his expensive but stinky stogie, Billy Vail said, "Other lawmen, federal, state, and county, have naturally raided all the wayside inns and rental properties the Dutch Uncle had amassed with the profits of crime. Need it be said nobody's cut the sign of Lachlan or Moran?"

Longarm flicked ashes, ignoring Vail's disapproving frown, as he said, "Both those old boys knew a thing or two about riding the Owlhoot Trail before Sand Lachlan ever tied in with the Dutch Uncle. He's no doubt at this minute using some of the suggestions the old priss made about not getting sloppy drunk in a strange town and steering clear of the whorehouses and seedy hotels the local law keeps its eye on."

"So which way did they go?" asked Vail.

To which Longarm could only reply, "East, west, north, or south. Riding together or traveling solo. With all the crooks they were working with dead or under arrest, it ain't as if they'll be looking over their shoulders as the piss runs down their legs. The question before the house is how much traveling money they have to work with. If they're short, they'll break cover sooner. If they have enough to lay low indefinite, then it figures to take us an indefinite amount of time to cut their trail."

Vail grumbled, "Thanks a heap. Never might have figured that out. So we shove the two that got away on the back of the stove for now and wait for them to strike again?"

Longarm said, "There's a couple of bets we haven't

176

covered. Lachlan told his gang he'd been forced to turn back at the border because that Apache scare had the crossing too heavily guarded. If he was telling the truth about that, he might have been telling the truth when he said all that hot paper had been left in an El Paso bank vault or mayhaps a hotel safe."

Vail said, "My opposite number from the El Paso District Court won't take long to check that out. We already have the hotel in El Paso and the name Lachlan registered under. Bank might take longer, but how many new accounts could anyone have opened in the days Lachlan was in town?"

He leaned back in his swivel chair to add, "I'll put Henry right on it. But what if Lachlan never cashed *anything* in El Paso on our side of the border?"

Longarm said, "It'll mean he sold the paper *south* of the border because he didn't act like a man who had anything on him to hide from his pals."

Vail nodded and said, "That works for me. We know Lachlan's a born double-crosser. So where do you figure he hid the cash if he unloaded all that hot paper without telling his pals, old son?"

Longarm said, "Don't know. Can't say for certain he did without talking to some low-life Mex money changers I know down yonder."

Vail grunted, "Then what are you waiting for, a kiss good-bye? Get your lazy ass down yonder, but stay on our side of the border as you see what you can find out. I mean that. These international incidents of yours are starting to be a bother!"

Without half-trying, the easygoing Longarm had made friends in places high and low down Mexico way. Some of them friends that would have upset *El Presidente* a heap, for the fatal flaw in all dictatorships is how much decent folks detest them, even those working for the government.

On the other hand, with that price on his head south of the border, a gringo lawman whose own boss had ordered him to stay the hell out of Old Mexico had to be careful about making *new* friends.

But Romero the money changer had done right in the past by rebel pals who vouched for him, and so Longarm, having to chance a meeting with *somebody* along the trail of those redeemed securities by way of Mexican money changers, met Romero in the back room of a cantina suggested as neutral ground near the Plaza del Toros in Ciudad El Paso Sur, which some bemused residents had recently taken to calling, against the frowns of El Presidente Diaz, Ciudad Juarez.

Romero was a short fat cuss with a sweaty face nearly as pale as his rumpled linen summer suit. It felt like shaking hands with pickled pig's knuckles.

As they sat across from one another at the blue-washed table with two clay mugs and a pitcher of *pulque* between them, Romero began by swearing, "As *Dios mio* knows to be true, I know nothing, nothing, of any robbery far to the north in your own country. I bought the paper in good faith at a . . . slight discount for to pay for my own time and trouble in redeeming them for cash in your country."

Longarm poured for the both of them as he said soothingly, "Like I asked them to tell you, Señor Romero, I don't have jurisdiction to do anything to anything or anybody down this side of the Rio Bravo. I'm only trying to confirm the picture I've put together of a bodacious double cross. I don't expect a gent in your line to tell me who unloaded a lot of hot paper on him for, say, a third its face value. I only have to know that in spite of all that gossip about the border being closed for another Apache scare, a couple of big fibbers had no trouble at all getting down this way with all that paper."

Romero gulped and said, "Forgive me, I am not feeling well. I fear you must excuse me for a *momento*."

As he rose from the table, Longarm said, "Aw, come on. I ain't after you for just doing what buzzards do down this way."

But Romero bolted out the back door, into the alley, as if he meant to throw up, and as Longarm gazed after him, the other door, in from the taproom, flew open and both Sand Lachlan and Frenchy Moran threw down on him as they came through it!

"I thought we locked that door behind us," said Longarm morosely.

Frenchy Moran aimed his Walker Conversion at Longarm's face as he let fly: "You two-faced rat! I trusted you and all the time you were lying to my face, and now I aim to shoot you right betwixt the eyes!"

Longarm nodded and said, "There's been a lot of that going around. You seem to trust two-faced rats beyond all reason, Frenchy. So before shooting me anywheres, would you care to hear how this *other* two-faced rat here cost you all that time in prison and cost you your Hazel as well?"

Sand Lachlan cocked his Schofield and snarled, "*Adios*, fucker!"

But then Frenchy ballet-kicked the .45 clean out of Lachlan's hand to land in a corner as Frenchy snapped, "Not so fast! What was that about *Hazel*?"

"She was waiting for you," Longarm replied without going into how he knew. He added, "You missed a lot of it because your pard here peached you to the law in Dodge so's *he* could try his luck with your Hazel."

"That's a fucking lie!" protested Lachlan.

Frenchy said, "I sure hope so. Keep talking, Doc, or should I call you Longarm?"

Longarm said, "Call me anything but late for breakfast. Starting at the beginning, before he'd screwed the rest of your bunch, Sand got you out of the way, but Hazel stayed true to you. I got it from Skippy that she'd turned him down and been relegated to less disgusting but way more dangerous chores by the time Sand here hooked up with the Dutch Uncle to pull off that big-ass robbery up Colorado way, where I *do* have some jurisdiction."

Sand Lachlan demanded, "Kill him, Frenchy! Don't you see what he's trying to do?"

Frenchy replied, "Sure I see what he's trying to do. Now hesh up and let me hear him out, unless you'd care to explain again how come you sent my poor pretty Hazel out into the Jornado del Muerto with Skippy to help Shadow Manners get away."

When Sand didn't answer, Frenchy told Longarm to keep going. So Longarm replied, "I got a better question. Why did *anyone* in your gang have to go help Shadow Manners? Why was Shadow Manners sent to murder another member of your own bunch in the first place?"

Frenchy murmured, "Sand?"

Lachlan said, "Shit, how many times do we have to go over that? Much as it pained me, once the law had poor Clem, we had to shut Clem up before he could talk!"

"About what?" asked Longarm mildly, never having felt so much like having a sip of half-ass *pulque* before. With his mouth dry as flannel, he tried to sound sarcastic as he continued. "He wasn't worried about a thing old Clem could have told the law. *I'm* the law, and we were riding that night train together when Shadow Manners shot him. Took me all the way to Cheyenne to figure out why. Can I have a sip of *pulque,* Frenchy?"

Frenchy said, "No. Keep talking, you two-faced rat!"

180

Longarm did. He said, "Speaking of two-faced rats, you were still in prison when the gang lit out from Colorado with all that hot paper. So it was Sand here and his *segundo,* Clem Aherne, who came here, with the others holed up north of the border, whilst they made the run south to fence the bonds and securities. You with me so far?"

Frenchy said, "I am. Keep talking."

Longarm said, "The way it reads best, the two of them agreed to fuck the rest of the gang out of their fair shares by saying they couldn't get across the border. So they had to cache the paper in El Paso. But then, being a two-faced hog as well as a two-faced rat, Sand turned Clem in to the law and had him hauled off the stage. Then he told the rest of the gang it was time to blue-streak back to Kansas."

Sand Lachlan wailed, "That's a fucking lie! Clem was my best pal!"

Longarm nodded soberly and said, "That's how come you found it so easy to fuck him. It's real easy to fuck folk who trust you. Once you handed him over to us, knowing he still knew you'd cashed the hot paper and hid the real money aside in El Paso, you hired Shadow Manners to kill Clem, and then you hired Alejandro Duran to kill Shadow, Skippy, and your Hazel in turn to drag red herrings across any flaws in the trail of lies you'd fed the rest of your gang."

He let that sink in and added, "But the best-laid plans of rats and men gang aft aglae, and here we are with all our dirty linen hanging out. I was there when Alejandro shot Skippy and a steambath sissy he took for Shadow. I'd shot Shadow earlier, and pretty little Hazel never made it as far as your death trap."

Frenchy asked, in a voice so strained he sounded like

an old lady, "Do you know what really happened to my Hazel? No bullshit, damn it!"

Longarm bleakly replied, "I was there too. Hazel fell off a cliff as she, Skippy, and me were riding over the San Andres. Wasn't the fault of anyone but this peerless leader of yours who sent a gal who wouldn't fuck out on a man's mission in rough country."

Then staring into the eyes of Mister Death himself, Longarm asked Frenchy to hold his fire till he'd heard the whole story.

Frenchy said, "I'm listening."

Longarm said, "You just got out. Thanks to me, you never got to take part in the big robbery I nipped in the bud. Even if I had jurisdiction south of the border, I'd have no serious federal offenses to charge you with. You weren't there when Sand here was being such a bad boy."

He let that sink in, and added, "This is a rough-and-ready town, policed by rough and ready *pistoleros* who'll come running if they hear gunplay."

Frenchy asked in a surprisingly studious tone, "What if I never used no gun and left town sneaky then?"

Longarm soberly replied, "What happens south of the border is none of my beeswax. On the other hand, if I never make it *north* of the border, my outfit will make it their beeswax to come looking for me, no matter where you might be headed from here."

Frenchy nodded and decided, "You'd best get along north of the border whilst we're both ahead then."

As Longarm rose to head for the alley door, Sand Lachlan wailed, "Hold on! I give up! I confess! Take me with you! For can't you see this foot-fighting maniac means to crunch me underfoot like a cockroach?"

To which Longarm could only reply as he turned in

the doorway with an amiable smile, "Sure I can. But if you ask me, it's about time somebody or the other crunched you underfoot like a cockroach, and like I keep saying, I just don't have the jurisdiction."

Watch for

LONGARM AND THE MONTANA MADMEN

308th novel in the exciting LONGARM series
from Jove

Coming in July!